Praise for
DONNA JO NAPOLI'S
Sirena

★ "The prose moves fluidly and the chapters flow smoothly into one another. . . . Secondary characters are clearly drawn yet retain a sense of distance that enhances the story's mythic aspects. . . . YAs will fall under the spell of [Sirena's] siren song and eagerly await [Napoli's] next foray into reimagined fantasy. It is also likely that the book will encourage readers to seek out the myths and literature that inspired it."

— *School Library Journal*, starred review

"Napoli unfurls a glorious story of love. . . . Fans of Greek mythology will enjoy [the] tales woven throughout, but it's the timeless, entrancing love story — the heartache, the triumph, and the bittersweet ending—that grabs the heartstrings."

— *Kirkus Reviews*

"Napoli's tale is rich in insight, fine language, and a look at truth told aslant. It is full of the sweetness of longing, romance, and the space and togetherness needed for any close relationship."

— *Booklist*

"Napoli has a firm grasp of things mythic and magical, and her ability to fuse active fantasy with emotional reality results in a well-realized world inhabited by emotionally true characters. Readers with a yen for an original take on tragic love may embrace this seaworthy expedition."

— *Bulletin of the Center for Children's Books*

"A strong female protagonist, the lure of myth, and enduring themes of love, honor, and vengeance combine in this powerful story by Napoli. . . . Readers will be absorbed by this beautifully-written book; many will be moved to seek out the myths and poetry that inspired it."

— *Voice of Youth Advocates*

An ALA Best Book for Young Adults
New York Public Library Book for the Teen Age

Other Signature Titles

When She Was Good
Norma Fox Mazer

Katarína
Kathryn Winter

The Music of Dolphins
Karen Hesse

Out of the Dust
Karen Hesse

SIRENA

DONNA JO NAPOLI

SCHOLASTIC
Signature

AN IMPRINT OF
SCHOLASTIC INC.

New York Toronto London Auckland Sydney
Mexico City New Delhi Hong Kong

FOR EMILY, WITH LOVE

ISBN 0-590-38389-2

Copyright © 1998 by Donna Jo Napoli.
Cover painting copyright © 1998 by Rafal Oblinski.
All rights reserved.
Published by Scholastic Inc.
SCHOLASTIC and associated logos are
trademarks and/or registered trademarks of Scholastic Inc.

12 11 10 9 8 7 6 5 4 3 2 1   0 1 2 3 4 5/0

Printed in the U.S.A.   40

First Scholastic Trade paperback printing, November 2000

Design by Elizabeth B. Parisi

Map by Elena Furrow

Acknowledgments

So many people made comments
on earlier versions of this story:
my family, Shannon Allen, Brenda Bowen,
Wendy Cholbi, Shelagh Johnston,
Hilary Kolton, Rachel Merz, Lucia Monfried,
Luisa Munson, Noëlle Paffett-Lugassy,
Ramneek Pooni, Emily Rando, Eric Ross,
Bob Schachner, Rachel Spear,
Stephanie Strassel, Richard Tchen,
William Kupprion and his Latin II class at
Strath Haven High School, fall 1996.
Thank you all.
A special thanks goes to Rosaria Munson,
who encouraged me not to abandon this story,
and to Linda Alter with her
Leeway Foundation, who gave me a boost
when I needed it.

Rhi

Pillars of Hercules

Carthage

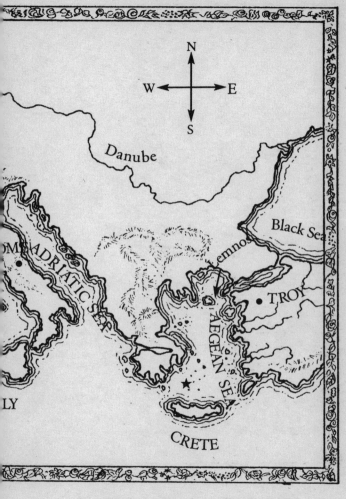

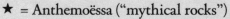

★ = Anthemoëssa ("mythical rocks")

SIRENA

DECEPTION

PART I

ONE

S
H
I
P
S

I am waiting, impatient and excited.

A glimpse of orange in the damp sand above the water's edge catches my eye. It is a dried starfish. That makes the fourth one I have found this week. I lace my hair around it. My sister Cecilia will be jealous. She has covered herself with starfish. And Pontina has taken over the mussel shells, stringing them around her neck in layers. Leila collects pearls. Her hands are red and pink with scrapes from fighting oysters. We make ourselves beautiful.

Just a little while ago the three vultures, our guardians, returned to our island of Anthemoëssa from a morning of surveying. The birds told us of a ship.

A ship! Within this day, a ship will be here.

A ship means human men. We are seventeen years old now. All ten of us. And these days our fondest desire is to be in the company of men. Last year another ship came close and our songs were sweet as the gods' nectar. When we paused for breath, we heard the men speaking of us with desire. They were drunk on our songs. Soon they would wreck on our reef. Soon they would swim into our arms.

Then a different song came — louder and more insinuating. The song of a lyre played by a master. My heart swirled on a melody that could raise the dead from Hades' underworld. Rocks from our island's highest peaks rolled into the sea to be closer to that lyre. The lilies, the only plants that grow on Anthemoëssa, strained on their stalks toward the music. We sang, desperation making our songs keen, but our voices were drowned by that magnificent and terrible lyre. At one point the music stopped and we heard a shout: "Play on, Orpheus!" The music played on. No matter how much we sang our hearts out, the men could no longer hear us. They passed us by.

Another time five of us tried to meet men as they

stood on shore. It was near the Italian city of Croton. The men looked at us in disbelief, fascination, then disgust. They lifted nets and harpoons. I go cold at the memory.

But today will be different. Shipwrecked on our island, the men of this ship will have time to know us better. Time to look beyond our crossbred outer selves and fall in love. For we have pure hearts and men of honor discern that. We are lovable.

Our guardian birds told us this ship was still too far away for the men to hear us. And since the ship is directly on course, we decided to delay singing until the last moment, for we must not exhaust ourselves in song. Love takes energy; I blush at the thought.

We have gone our various ways to wait. Mermaids cluster, combing one another's hair, stringing shells for necklaces and bracelets and cinches, picking lilies and tying them with bunches of seaweed to their tails in an effort to cover all but their lovely brown breasts. We know our tails are our enemies. They always have been.

"Come!" Cecilia calls with urgency. "I see the ship."

We gather quickly — none of us has gone far. We swim around the island to where it rises in a sheer cliff. We go to our favorite singing rock offshore. I climb deftly, using my horizontal tail fin as a foot, and find my place among my sisters.

The men are almost here. My heart pounds. We sing in harmony, in rounds, in unison. We sing chants and melodies.

> *Come to us, wayfaring sailor*
> *Come and be satiated*
> *Drink the sweet wine*
> *Eat all the fruits*
> > *Quicken your spirit*
> *Come to us, wayfaring sailor*
> *Come be enlightened*
> *Listen and learn*
> *Know all the past*
> > *Know all the future*
> *Come to us, wayfaring sailor*
> > *Come, come, come*

Our voices weave the invisible net. Our three guardian birds turn their heads to us in approval.

The surface of my entire body stings with anticipation. I am as convinced by our song as the sailors must be. Oh, yes, there is a man on that ship who will be my love. Mine.

I smell the ship before I see it. These men are on a long voyage. They have packed crates of food, amphoras of wine. The wood of the ships is piney. The sweat of the men is sour. I smell their shoes, their dirty hair, smells I recognize from the one long day I spent with land creatures, years ago, at Thetis' wedding. Heady smells.

And, oh, I smell too much for how far away the ship still is. The West Wind has woken. He blows our song back into our throats. No! The men in the ship won't be able to hear us. Who has shaken Zephyr, that naughty wind, from his bed in Aeolia?

Now Notos, the South Wind, picks up. Notos is strong and hot, coming across the sands of Africa. He blows the ship northward. Away from us. Away! We sing into the wind, half shouting in defiance. We do not fool ourselves: The ship is on another course. Gone.

My sisters stop singing, one after the other. We stare out to sea.

Sadness washes away thought. The emptiness of the horizon mesmerizes. Noon sun beats on our heads.

At last the skin of my arms and face calms. I look around at the deadened faces of my sisters. I need to shake off this gloom. "It's almost time for the squid to rise. Let's swim out to the deepest waters and watch."

Alma scowls at me. "Your cheerfulness annoys, Sirena."

I move till our sides touch. When the squid shoot up

into the air, it is thrilling. Their skin lets off an internal light. Their eyes show bliss. "Let's go. Please."

Alma furrows her brow in worry. "You've been too close to them again, haven't you? Squid are the fastest predators of the sea. If they see you are alone, they could turn on you in an instant."

"When they leave the water, they are so entranced, they cannot notice me."

"Someday you will pay for your independence, Sirena. Squid are too stupid to think of anything but food." Alma tosses her hair. "But I don't want to argue now. Hush."

My sisters call all mollusks and fish and crustaceans and reptiles stupid, as though there is no difference between the thoughtless herring and the cunning squid. They think we are higher creatures. They revel in the fact that we must rise from the depths for breath, like the porpoise. They shed tears often, just to prove we have lacrimal glands, unlike fish. They show their breasts in pride; they think we are live-bearers who would suckle our young. But not one of us has had a chance to find out if that is so.

I swim off. The winds have died. The water flattens.

But, oh, our guardian birds fly toward us once more. I hadn't even noticed they had left our island. They fly with purpose; they tell us of three ships. Three! All on their way to Anthemoëssa. How can this be? A whole year without a ship, then four on one day? We swirl in the water, gleeful.

"Hurry," says Iole.

We climb the rock. We sing with the clarity of glass bells. We will sing until our throats are raw. This time we will not fail.

I spy the first ship. It is larger than the one Notos blew off course at midday. It must carry many men.

The ship comes closer. And the second one, too. Now we see all three. The men wave to us, dark hair sprouting on their faces.

A wind rises. Nasty Rhodope, the sea nymph who hates all mermaids, must be calling in her favors. But the ships are too close now for winds to foil our plan. The men have seen us. They have seen women with naked breasts and flowers and pearls in their flowing hair. Our songs captivate them. They pull down their lone sail and heave at the oars and conquer the waves. Rhodope cannot win this time.

We sing and sing.

The winds blow in every direction. It is a veritable storm.

The ships bear down, straight toward Anthemoëssa, perfectly in line with the underwater ridge that, within moments, will tear their wooden planks.

We sing.

Crack! The first ship rips apart on the ridge. The men of the second ship shout to one another. They push on the oars and try to change the course of the ship, but it is lost. *Crack!* The second ship rips asunder. The men of the third ship scream frantically. They join forces, three men to an oar on the right side of the ship and, wonder of wonders, they manage to turn the ship. They hoist the sail and the wind carries them away. The men in the water call to them. Their calls sound like gull cries.

We are sad to see the third ship sail away, but we rejoice at the wreckage of the first two. We laugh and wait shyly. What will a first kiss taste like? I don't dare to think beyond a kiss. The skin on my arms prickles at imagined pleasure. I lick my lips.

But only a few men swim toward shore. Where are the others? There is commotion in the water, though the waves have died down as suddenly as they arose. There are screams and thrashings.

The horror hits us like a slap: These men don't know how to swim!

I dive and go as fast as I can to the first man I find. He is short and thin. He doesn't struggle. I cannot feel the rise and fall of his chest. I hold onto the man with one arm. I pull him toward the rocks, using all my strength to go fast and faster. His head lolls on his neck. I hold it in place on my shoulder with my chin. It is so hard to keep his nose and mouth out of the water. Oh, cursèd high rocks. This man is much too heavy for me to lift. And this side of the island has no beach. I am forced to swim around to the side that offers a pebbled inlet. I drag the man out of the water until his head rests in the open air. I touch his face. It is cold as fish. I put my hand under his nose. No heat comes. I breathe into his mouth and pound on his chest. Nothing. I cry hot tears on his cheeks. I shout in his gaping mouth.

My sisters cry and shout around me in rising agony. The inlet is strewn with human bodies and grieving mermaids. The sound shatters the air. I twist my hands in my hair and pull.

No. This cannot be. Never. I enter the water defiantly and swim back to the underwater ridge. I dive and search. There must be others alive yet. I will save them.

I dive again. And again. But more slowly now, for I know that if I find anything, it will be cold as fish.

In the end, eleven men survive. Six of them swam to shore. The other five clung to pieces of wreckage until my sisters and I rescued them. Eighteen lie dead on the beach. Eighteen men no longer breathe. And more were stolen by the underwater currents. More dead. My own breath comes only with great effort.

The survivors huddle together and watch us with eyes that speak. They fear us; they blame us.

But we are not to blame. No. How could we have known they didn't swim? How could these men have been so foolhardy as to climb into ships when they didn't know how to swim? We shed tears over their limp hairy bodies. We line them up, side by side. Innocent men. Dead men. Dead, dead, dead.

I sit beside one. Not the man I pulled from the water. Just a man. All of the dead are equal. My tears fall on his feet. His shoes were lost in the water. His toes are white with coarse black hairs on the top. The nails are long and gnarled. My eyes travel up his thick calves. As a man he was strong. But as a fish, he was weaker than a minnow.

The survivors have clambered across the rocks and come through the center of the island to the inlet. They stand as a group now. One of them steps forward. "Get away! Get away from him!" he shouts at me.

I push off into the water and watch from a distance. My sisters are in the water with me.

The man looks out over us. His look is fierce. My sisters throng together. We make our faces soft as sponges. We give sweet looks.

"What kind of unnatural spirits are you?" He marches to the dead and stands over them possessively.

"Stay away." He glares. His hair drips. His wet shirt clings to his warm chest. The water has nearly undone him. His voice alone is strong. He is piteous.

Our tears add salt to the sea.

This man motions to the other survivors. They march to the center of the island where the ground is flat — where my sisters and I used to roll when we were small, pretending to be land animals. The men dig with bare hands. The dirt on Anthemoëssa is only a thumb deep. The men hit solid rock. They curse and move to another spot. The scene repeats.

The leader turns and walks back to the line of bodies in the inlet. "Come, men. We must pull them up above the water level at high tide, so they don't get washed away. We will find a way to bury them."

The men drag the bodies to higher ground. Then they walk out of sight.

We swim in circles, listlessly. It has all gone wrong. We must make these eleven men understand that we didn't know the others couldn't swim. We must make them forgive us. We must make them love us.

The men return to the inlet. Instantly we sing, our voices ropes of anguish, but if anything can win them, it is our song.

"Silence!" The leader picks up a loose rock. "There is

no fresh water on this island. There are no animals except three vultures. There are no plants but lilies. This is an uninhabitable island. A hell above ground." He throws the rock. It splashes in our midst. "Damn you! Damn all of you! You think you have won." He picks up another rock and throws it as hard as he can. "We should have listened to the men of the *Argo*. They warned us of singing birds. But no one told us of you. They must not have seen you. Of course not. Anyone who sees you dies. The Argonauts thought the birds sang — but it was your song. You. Wretched misshapen monsters of the deep. Seductresses of evil."

"No!" I shout. "No. We are not that way."

"Silence!" he screams again. "Do not speak. Do not sing. We will allow no more treachery." He presses his open hands against his cheeks and looks to the skies. "Oh, gods, have pity on us. Help us escape." He picks up another rock and looks around at the survivors. They, too, pick up rocks. We are showered with the rocks of their hatred.

TWO

T
E
A
R
S

They carry rocks with them everywhere. They say if we come close, they will kill us; if we speak, they will kill us. Right now they are walking to the rocky side of the island, the side facing the ridge their ships crashed on. Two of them turn out to be strong swimmers. They go in search of wreckage that might be rebuilt into a smaller ship — a boat — even a raft. Their efforts are valiant. But most of the boards were smashed into pieces too small to be useful. And much has been lost in the underwater currents.

When they rest, we help. We gather every bit of rope and board and cloth we find and pile them on the rocks, as close to the men as we dare. Then we back away. The men eye our pile with suspicion. Finally one of them sifts through the rubble. He calls over the others. They sigh.

As dark comes, the men retreat to the inner part of the island. We take to the lower rocks on the cliff side.

Dreams of terror fill the first night.

In the morning some of them try fishing. To no avail. They mutter about the loss of nets. We search the waters for nets, but none are found.

The men pass the day eating snails and clams from the intertidal pools. The two good swimmers go in search of wreckage again, but find nothing at all. The men curse the hot sun, then beg forgiveness of Helios, the sun god. They pray to Zeus for rain. They find old conch shells and turn them open-side up, hopeful receptacles for rain. We dive and search and Alma finds an empty tortoise shell. She puts it on the beach. We watch as the leader examines the shell without touching it. He looks out at us with confusion on his face, then snatches up the shell.

The second night the moon is still bright. Our guardian birds fly restlessly about the highest peak of Anthemoëssa. The men throw rocks at them. Their nightmares are loud.

In the morning one of the good swimmers makes a crude spear from a splintered board. He walks into the water shouting that he will stab us in the heart if we come near. He dives.

The others wait, tensely holding rocks and looking at us. Their red skin peels. Their dry lips crack. They breathe with open mouths, fat tongues showing. I scan the sky: no rain clouds. This time of year it rarely rains. "Eat the lilies," I shout, breaking the ban these men have put on our speech. "The lilies hold liquid."

Cecilia's head appears out of the water. "Help! Come quick!" We dive after her, around the underwater hill. Immediately I recognize the octopus den from the pile of crab shells outside. My heart clutches as I guess. And I am right: The man's hunger made him reckless. His spear lies broken on the sea bottom. The octopus has twined around him. The man doesn't struggle. The octopus blushes in anger at our approach. He releases the body and curls into his den.

We pull the body to shore and let Cecilia drag it up on the beach while we swim back out and hover. Cecilia leans over the body. She wails softly.

The other ten men are scattered here and there. One of them springs from behind a rock and runs toward Cecilia. He grabs her hair and pulls her up onto the dirt where we rarely go. She cries out. Within moments the others have come. They slam rocks on her. They smash her head and ribs.

We scream, helpless in the sea. If we go on land, they will kill us. But staying in the water is hideous. We scream and scream until I cannot hear my own shrieks any longer.

The leader throws armfuls of lilies on Cecilia's blood-stained hair. "Vicious whore from hell!" He spits on what was once her face.

We are shocked into silence.

The leader turns to us and shouts, "Horrid flowers. You grow them to deceive sailors into thinking this rock of an island welcomes them. Then you entreat us to eat them. They are poison to our souls. Stay away or we will kill you all and bury you with flowers."

His words come as if from a great distance. They seem unreal.

These men are doomed.

My sister is dead.

Everything is wrong.

I swim and swim. Even though I am large and swift, it is dangerous for me to be alone in the sea at night. I should climb onto a rock. But I see none and I no longer know where I am. I have lost my bearings. And, oh, that is how I want it to be. I refuse to look for signs of land. I swim in the moonlight.

As dawn comes, my exhaustion wins. I float and cry.

I pass a small island covered with monk seals that hop around, shifting their weight from front flippers to tail fin in a clumsy lope. A bull swims near with a pup on his head. I think of the camaraderie of my sisters, my school. I turn my face away.

For days I wander. I swim and eat and rest. I never think, never remember. I do not even worry about being eaten.

I go nowhere.

Night after day, day after night. Nowhere.

Or, I thought I was going nowhere, but now, as evening prepares to fall, I see our three guardian birds in triple flight overhead. I have made a giant circle: My primordial fish instinct prevails, carrying me home. I hesitate, then lick the salt water on my lips — the water that is my companion for life. I consent to the inevitable and swim to Anthemoëssa.

When I am still far from shore, I smell the stench. The human bodies are piled on rocks offshore. Our guardian birds pick at the rotting flesh. Our island, which was once a mass of fragrant yellow lilies, has become an open graveyard. Not a single flower lifts its face to the sun.

"Sirena. Oh, Sirena." Alma swims up and we hug each other. "I didn't know what had happened to you."

"Are they all dead?"

"Yes," she whispers.

Alma holds me as I sob. Then she leads me to the rock where I used to sit with the sisters I have lived with all my life. We were ten before; we are but nine now.

"We waited for you," says Iole. "It hurts when you go off without us. We looked out to sea, morning, noon, and night."

I understand and I am at once sorry for having left them like that. We are a school of mermaids; we find solace in numbers. I belong with them.

I sleep with my sisters on the warm rock of my childhood.

THREE

S
T
O
R
I
E
S

The green-brown turtle swims beside me at the bottom of shallow waters. Morning light penetrates the bay. The turtle navigates by sunlight. We use the siltiness of the sea bottom, the saltiness of the water.

We have been swimming the whole day long, ever since Lavinia woke us. Our guardian birds announced to her that Mother Dora visits our sea — she is already in her grotto, she awaits us. Mother Dora, the wife of Nereus, the Old Man of the Sea, and the daughter of Oceanus himself. Mother Dora, the wonderful storyteller, who has always been good to us. We swim toward Mother Dora, knowing she will tell us the story of our origin — the story we love to hear over and over — hoping the very storytelling itself will comfort us in our grief.

We pass over the ruins of a town that a terrible earthquake left flooded forever. I would rest in the ancient home below if I could. I would pick up pieces of pottery and dream about the human families. But it is near evening. We must hurry. I swim close to the turtle and dream of clasping onto her shell like a limpet and traveling far out into the wide waters of the world.

The massive sea turtle has been swimming several times longer than I, yet she shows no sign of exhaustion. She has come from beyond the great rock that is home to many apes, beyond the Pillars of Hercules and the strait that leads to the endless waters ruled by Oceanus. She bites off huge clumps of grass with heavy jaws. Her front legs are flat and elongated, like oars from a ship. Her hind feet are wide. She sculls along easily.

Mother Dora looks over the assembly in the grotto. She is not related to mermaids, but she is as close to a relative as we have ever had. Her face is kind. For a moment I wish Mother Dora were our real mother. But, then, the dreaded nymph Rhodope would be my sister. "Ten mermaids are missing — an entire school." Her regal voice carries through the waters melodically. I lean forward in reverence. Mother Dora is the mother of all the sea nymphs. She is used to counting to fifty, for there are fifty sea nymphs, just as there were fifty mermaids — before Cecilia was killed. She raises a questioning eyebrow, her face full of concern. We realize at once that she already knows of Cecilia's death and she fears for the other ten missing mermaids. Perhaps our guardian birds told her, for none of us would dare speak unless she addressed us first.

We look around. The nymph Amphitrite appears beside me. She opens her mouth to speak and air bubbles escape. "The ten from the north river are not coming, Mother."

A pang of loss strikes. Usually after Mother Dora leaves, the five schools of mermaids sit on the island of Ischia and have singing contests. Our river sisters win. We used to say they would be the first to have success with human men.

Mother Dora accepts their absence with a nod, then turns to us. "This is a grim time, my charming mermaids."

Tears come to our eyes. The other schools of mermaids look at us. They know, too. Their eyes, too, fill with tears.

"Grim, indeed. After our storytelling, all of you will

return together to Anthemoëssa. Mourn your sister as one. But you must remember that you are unique. You make the waters you inhabit special above all the other waters of the world." Mother Dora has often told us this. She makes us feel extraordinary — chosen.

Mother Dora lifts her arms toward us, signaling the start to our story. I am surprised. I want her to say more about Cecilia. I want her to cry with us.

Her eyes settle on the nymph beside me. "You, Amphitrite, are superb. A fitting wife for King Poseidon, who rules this sea and the Friendly Sea, as well as the underground rivers."

Amphitrite looks pleased. Her pleasure warms the water.

Now Mother Dora looks at the nymph behind Alma. "You, Thetis, are magnificent. You and King Peleus are the proud parents of young Achilles, whose fame will endure."

Thetis stands tall, rigid. Her tension radiates. It penetrates the thickness of our sorrow — but we do not understand.

Mother Dora looks around one more time. Those are the only nymphs who have come today. "All my nymph daughters are lovely. But Rhodope, we must admit, is the daring nymph." Mother Dora pauses. "Daring brings rewards." She looks directly at me. "And costs."

My cheeks burn. I swallow the lump in my throat. I hold myself still as an oyster; my innards work around Mother Dora's unspoken warning like an oyster's around a grain of sand.

"It was that daring nature that led Rhodope to travel out of sea waters, into the open ocean waters that circle the earth." Mother Dora's hands dance. "She traveled to the distant giant island where she found the coral reef and, within a crevice, the slumbering parrot fish." Her fingers vibrate down her body. "The parrot fish, your mother, shimmered in blues: sky blue and sea blue and blood blue. She shimmered in greens on her side fins, and purples on her dorsal fin. Her belly was pink-purple. Above and below her mouth were clean white stripes."

I imagine our mother sleeping. Were her lidless eyes circled with yellow? In the past Mother Dora has told us our mother's scales looked as if their edges had been dipped in gold.

"Rhodope named this fish Little Iris, after the goddess of the rainbow. She put her in a cage." Mother Dora moves in and out among us, walking as easily as on land. Water and air are the same to her. She is so much like a human woman, but she is immortal, as are all gods.

Mother Dora smiles. "Eros, that randy god of desire and love, was waiting for Rhodope when she returned from her travels." Mother Dora laughs. She has a soft spot for Eros. I have never met our father. Yet from what I know of him, I never want to. "Eros made love with Rhodope." Mother Dora speaks with honeyed tongue. "Then while she slept, his roving eye fell on Little Iris." Mother Dora's eye roves among us like Eros' eye. I want to flee that eye. Did Little Iris want to flee her cage? Did she yearn for coral to hide in? At this moment I hate our father, as I always do at this point of the story.

"Eros seduced Little Iris. It didn't take much cleverness. Little Iris was stupid and mindless, like any other fish." Mother Dora wags her finger as if in warning. I cannot understand who she warns. "When Rhodope awoke, she saw Little Iris' eggs shining and realized what had happened. She swallowed the eggs." Mother Dora returns to the center of the assembly and stands perfectly still. "Little Iris watched calmly, in her unutterable dumbness. She didn't even know they were her eggs."

Mother Dora dwells today on our mother's stupidity in a way that grates. Of course a fish knows little. Why harp on it? A moon jellyfish happens into the grotto. It swims past my face with rhythmic contractions of its shallow bell. I watch, telling myself to calm down — there is no point in getting irritated. I must relax and let myself find solace in the storytelling, for that is what I need most. The giant turtle resting near the west wall of the grotto snaps just once — and the jellyfish is gone down her gullet.

"But, Eros, with help, saved one hundred eggs."

With help? Mother Dora has never spoken of this before. I turn my full attention to her again.

Mother Dora stretches out her hands, cupped together. "I joined Rhodope in eating the eggs." Aghast, we huddle together instinctively. "But instead of swallowing, I carried one hundred eggs on my tongue until Rhodope left, thinking she had triumphed. Then I spit them into Eros' hands."

So Mother Dora saved us. A murmur of realization and gratitude fills the grotto. Ah. We move closer to her, feeling the unity of all mermaids, of four schools merging into one.

"Rhodope learned of my deceit, of course. Eros is loose with all body parts — including his tongue. He is the most foolish god. In fact . . . " — Mother Dora looks around at us slowly — "it is amazing that you have any brains at all, with such parents."

My face and palms itch in anger at the insult. I look at my sisters. Confusion fills their eyes.

Mother Dora relents with a smile. "I tease." But Mother Dora's words come too late; her smile smacks of a mean spirit. "Rhodope cursed you then: Unlike fish, unlike gods, you are forbidden to couple with your brothers or your father."

The mention of our brothers adds a vague sadness to our pain. They were banished to Oceanus' waters the day Rhodope cursed us. Our guardian birds said they were eaten by a pod of killer whales in a sea where ice mountains float. My sisters cried. I drifted off alone and tried to imagine an ice mountain at sea. I could not, and in the deepest recesses of my heart I felt sure my brothers lived still. I feel that way now.

Mother Dora clears her throat. She says the terrible words we are waiting for: "And, like humans, you are mortal."

Mother Dora looks around. Her eyes gleam through the dim water. I beg her eyes to stop on me, just as each of my sisters does. Each wants to be the one to play the only other role in the storytelling. I am so tense, I rise on my tail without realizing what I do until I see my sisters doing the same.

Mother Dora points at a sister from another sea group. She is Uri. Oh, lucky Uri.

Uri shouts, "Unless . . . "

"Unless," says Mother Dora, lifting her right hand, "unless a human should become your mate. Only then would you gain immortality." She smiles. "And that is why I gave you the gift of song. With song you can win human love." She bows her head while the nymphs and mermaids blow bubbles of applause.

I do not applaud, though. I want to ask how song can help us, when men are such poor swimmers. The question torments me.

Mother Dora lifts her hands to signal it is time for her to yield the center to Amphitrite, who will regale us with a new story. Amphitrite tells tales of the gods — she is the source of our knowledge of how the world began and how it works. But, no, Mother Dora speaks again: "This is the most important time of your lives."

Her tone is grave. Her words surprise. My sisters and I listen intently.

"Thetis, come forward. Tell them."

Thetis walks to the center of the assembly, silvery-footed and slender. Her dress is red-pink. I have never understood this habit of gods and humans of covering their bodies, even though Mother Dora once explained to us about modesty. But I admire the beauty of fine clothing. Thetis looks splendid today. She is proud, yet the tension she exuded before remains. "Do you remember my wedding?"

Thetis' wedding is the only wedding we have ever been to; of course we remember. We sat in a pool dug specially for us. We ate the flesh of a land animal — lamb. It was exquisitely tender. We laughed and sang and watched the gods get drunk. Young Hermes splashed into our pool and we passed around his winged sandals and hat; we twirled his magic wand.

"Do you remember the apple of discord?"

An apple was thrown into the midst of the guests with a tag that read, "For the fairest." All the beautiful goddesses fought. We hid underwater in our pool in fear.

Thetis looks approvingly at our nodding heads. "Zeus, that crafty soul, refused to judge the fairest. He left it to the Trojan prince Paris, who chose Aphrodite."

This much I knew. Hera called her husband Zeus a coward for not acting as judge — for not choosing her.

Paris herded sheep on Mount Ida and was the nymph Oenone's lover. I envied Oenone, for she must have eaten lamb every day.

"In return Aphrodite promised Paris the most beautiful woman in the world: Helen, wife of Menelaus of Sparta. Paris stole Helen away to Troy." Thetis speaks softly. "All of Greece now bands together to fight Troy, so that Menelaus can have Helen back. They have worked for years building ships."

Mother Dora nods. "So, mermaids, my ready maidens, the seas are full of Greek ships heading for Troy. The first ships set sail last month." She smiles. "Ships carrying men."

We understand now: That's why four ships happened our way in only one day. Those were Greek warriors.

"You must not be stupid." Mother Dora's words catch us by surprise. "You are of age, my beauties. This war is your best opportunity. One thousand ships."

I do not understand. This war is no opportunity for us. I move toward Mother Dora, hoping her eyes will fall on me, hoping she will bid me speak.

Her eyes do fall on me. "I saved you, little mermaids," she says firmly. "Me. I protected you. Never forget that. Never forget that I know what's best for you. You mustn't act like idiot fish. You must do it perfectly."

I move closer yet to Mother Dora. I must ask exactly what we are to do.

But Mother Dora turns her eyes toward the others, dismissing me. "If you win lovers, my seas can be graced with mermaids forever. Beautiful mermaids to match my beautiful nymph daughters. Forever and ever." Mother Dora looks at us lovingly. "Immortality."

I close my eyes. I have envied every last god and goddess, from the great Titans down to the simple naiads that live in brooks. They never grow old. They cannot be killed.

But I don't understand how we mermaids can ever win immortality. I open my eyes. I can hardly contain my question.

"Go now, sweet mermaids," says Mother Dora.

"Wait!" I cry.

"Wait!" comes an echo. But, no, it is a louder voice than mine. A thin sea nymph slips out from the dark back of the grotto. No one had noticed her before. Her face is drawn.

"Oenone," says Thetis. "How frail you have become."

Oenone, the nymph that Paris lived with before he abandoned her for Helen. She wears misery as a cloak.

"Please," says Oenone. "Sweet mermaids, please. Stop not one ship of Greeks. Let them go to Troy and capture Paris." Her voice breaks. She finishes in a whisper. "Let them kill him."

We swim around one another in confusion. We want mates; we don't know how to win them; we don't want to hurt Oenone. We know nothing.

FOUR

W
A
R

I am awakened by the scream of our guardian birds. I have been napping in midday, like a seal. Thessa, a sister from another group, is the first to call out. "A ship."

I sigh. Ten days ago, before we wrecked those two ships, Thessa's words would have brought hope to my heart.

I rest my cheek back against the rock. These many days, with the four schools of mermaids living together, have helped relieve my sorrow. I sleep without nightmares once more.

I hear splashing, and look around. My sisters slide into the water from the surrounding rocks. They swim to meet the others in the sea. I do not understand. I join them.

"From the ridge side again," says Thessa.

"Everyone, sing," says Pontina. "Then, when I give the sign, we will go to our posts."

My sisters swim to the singing rocks.

"No!" I shout, in panic. "Pontina, what are we doing?"

The songs of my sisters rise, smooth and silky.

"No!" I swim around the rocks and shout up at them. "No! We cannot do this again."

Not one of them looks at me. Their strong voices compel.

I pull on Pontina's tail. She shakes me off. I pull on Alma's tail. She shakes it. I hold on tight and bite.

Alma slaps my face.

I fall away, stunned.

Uri reaches for me. "Climb up. Join us."

"What about Oenone?" I say.

Uri clicks her tongue against the roof of her mouth. "There are so many men. One thousand ships full. Surely the other men can kill Paris without the help of the few few men that we few few mermaids need."

I turn to Alma and grab her tail again. "Uri doesn't

know the horror. She wasn't with us when we wrecked the other ships. But you know, Alma. We can't do this."

"Don't make trouble, Sirena," says Alma. "We have plans."

"When did you make plans?"

"We talk often."

I shake my head. "I never heard you."

"You aren't always sensible. We talked when you swam away, after Cecilia's death. We talk each day as you sleep."

I cannot believe they would do that — I cannot believe they would leave me out. "The men will drown."

"We all have posts in the sea. When they come near the ridge, we will take our posts and save them. They will be grateful to us. They will love us."

I remember the hatred in the men's eyes, their cries of "monster." They will never love us. I look at the determined faces of my sisters. Desperation makes rigid lines on their necks, on their rib cages. "The men will die, Alma. They will die for lack of fresh water."

"We will sing continually. They will love us."

"Even if they love us, they will die."

Alma, the sweetest of my sisters, now looks at me with hard eyes. "They will love us first." She lifts her chin and sings.

I am stunned. I swim out and look across the whole group of mermaids. "Stop!" I shout. "Look what's happened. We have become the monsters they said we were."

But my sisters cannot hear me. They sing more temptingly than ever. Their need heightens the intensity. No man could resist songs so excruciatingly lovely.

I swim quickly. My sisters' songs show no sign of hesitation. Surely they realize what I am doing, but they sing a carefree, light song. I am above the underwater ridge now. I have reached it before the ship. Oh, yes, there is time. I shout to the men. "Turn away! Your lives depend upon it. Turn away!"

The men are at the oars, working. Sweat blinds them. The honey of mermaids' songs fills their ears. They neither see nor hear me.

And now my sisters' songs are louder. They have taken up their posts in the sea. The music seems to lift the ship along.

"Go back!" I scream. I grab onto an oar and hold with all my strength. "Save yourselves!"

The two men on the other end of this oar look at me. Their faces are dumbfounded. They shout to the others.

"Go back!" I scream.

My weight has upset the timing of the oars. An oar hits me on the back. Pain sears through my middle. I fall away, spinning under the ship. Blood coats my tongue. Somewhere in the back of my mind is the vague sense that I must stop something — but I cannot for the life of me know what. Another vague idea comes: If I lose consciousness, I could be underwater for a long time. I could drown. The thought makes me lightheaded.

The bottom of the ship goes straight into the ridge. The ship's boards rip apart. The men tumble into the water.

My lightheadedness is instantly gone.

I cry. I cry for Cecilia and the dead men. I cry for these men who think they are still alive. I cry for us all.

HONESTY

PART II

FIVE

L
e
m
n
o
s

I swim east. My body rides high in the night water.

There is an island where the first rays of sun bring sight to blind eyes. Orion went there to recover his sight — Orion, who ended up as stars, twinkling straight above in winter. It is summer now, but I know the direction of Orion's island. I do not need to follow the line of his sword. I am going there to find new sight. I will wipe from my brain the sights I have seen and start over. I must arrive at the island by dawn — in time for the first rays of sun.

For many years the island was inhabited by families. Then the women rose up against the men. Amphitrite told us the story. The women killed the men. Every last one of them, except the old king. They put him in a chest and set him afloat on the sea. The waves carried him to a distant shore. He wandered from town to town telling the people, the birds, the trees, the air — anyone, anything that would listen — of the murders he had seen. For this reason no man visits the island.

It is the island of Lemnos. I will live the rest of my life there. I will never see humans. I can think of no safer place to go. I need an island's coves in a storm; I need an island's offshore rocks for sleeping.

As I swim now, I am aware of every part of my body. My fingers are long with nails white as the insides of clamshells. My neck is thin like the stalks of the lilies that grew on Anthemoëssa. My breasts are warm and smooth as porpoise belly. Then my fish half begins. My scales flash when light touches them. My colors suit the seas. The spine that runs full length within me is sharp and supple.

I will feed this body — this strange mixture — the nourishment it needs, for it houses me.

But it will never know love. The stirrings of lust I had not long ago — those barest stirrings, those smallest hopes — they must die forever.

Just as I will die.

For if I knowingly killed a man, how could I want to go on living? I trade immortality for the right to want to live.

This is Rhodope's doing, I am sure of it. She foresaw all. She orchestrated the tragedy. Her intent was to make every mermaid hideous and hateful.

I shout into the wind, "Look at me, whoever cares. Feast your eyes." Rhodope, unwittingly to be sure, has given me the greatest gift of all: I know myself totally for the first time. I am mermaid — hybrid and mortal. I am a monster in body, like the shipwrecked men said. But I am decent in soul.

Calm envelops me like a warm, slow current.

A school of mackerel surrounds me. They are silver fast. I realize I can see their color; a predawn glow infiltrates the sea. I must hurry. I wave my arms at the mackerel and they dart away and quickly back again. Now they dive, and I see why: Big blue jellyfish float up ahead. Their stinger-studded tentacles extend my body's length or more under the water. I am grateful to the mackerel for the warning.

I dive after the school. When I surface, Lemnos rises before me, a magnificent high, rocky face. I spy a dark spot near the top — a cave. I swim to a rock not far from a gently inclined beach. I climb up and rest on my stomach, facing east. The first sparks from Helios' chariot shoot out as he rides across the sky. I roll onto my back. I want to believe this sunrise will purify my sight. I want to believe I will once more be innocent as fish. I close my eyes.

I wake to the sound of roosters, remnants of the human inhabitants. I explore the outer shallows of this stretch of island. There is no need to see the whole island quickly. I have plenty of time. I have the rest of my life.

A grotto gleams emerald in the afternoon sun. It is wider than Mother Dora's and shallower; the sun penetrates the waters easily. I find a human home built on a beach. The roof has collapsed. I am not tempted to explore it. In part, because I don't want to be vulnerable to whatever animals prowl the island. In part, because I no longer want to know human things.

Days pass.

I enjoy details. A parade of lobsters, each holding on with a claw to the tail of the one in front. A family of albatrosses. Many families of diving birds. Fighting gulls with brown heads and orange beaks and black tips on their wings.

Waves here can be high. Three, four times my body length. I learn to ride the highest. I could almost laugh.

The wind blows continuously in the same direction — in toward my beach. The wind stirs the waves.

Day after day.

A bear growls one morning. Perhaps he lives in the cave on the cliff. Perhaps Orion slew his ancestors. The coo of doves coddles me at dusk. Leopards scream at night.

I am aware of dawn and noon and evening and night. But I don't keep track.

One late afternoon a shark glides by me as I swim. There are many sharks in these waters, but they are small and no threat. This one is long. He could eat me if he wanted. I retreat to a rock, my breath solid and quick.

I am mortal and always will be.

Anger comes hard. If I yield to fear, my life will become small and dry, until no pleasures touch me at all. I must allow myself adventure.

I take a breath and dive, heading for deep sea. I don't have to search long — I sense what I am after. The evening light weakens as I spin down toward the rising school of squid below. Excitement crawls along my spine, teasing like tiny crab legs. The water is frigid this deep, even though it is summer above. It tastes more of salt. I shiver. Danger pulses around me. The water is full of noise and motion. The squid school below must be immense, maybe the largest I've ever known. My heart-beat speeds.

All at once they are here, propelling in wild profusion, greening the waters with their inner light. Some shoot past so fast, I spin.

A few tunas, huge, shine silver in the squid light. They swim swiftly by. The school of squid turns almost as a unit. They chase, voracious and relentless.

I think of Alma's admonition long ago — if the tunas get away, the squid may hunt me. I sought adventure, not death. I head for the edge of the hungry school. My teeth clench; my jaw aches with tension.

But the squid turn again, as if some message has been passed through the water, back to their original course. Squid shoot into me and I am pushed upward again. Nothing matters to them now but the rise — I sense this and relief makes my muscles soft once more. We move faster than I have ever moved alone. Their sinuous arms brush my sides and chest. I forget everything; I cannot think. I feel only this rush. Faster and faster. This thrilling rush.

I fight the water and force my head back until I luxuriate in squid arms all over my face. I am like Medusa, the Gorgon of one of my favorite stories — but with squid hair instead of snake. The water presses hard. I tighten, ready.

At last we rocket out of the water, high and free in the hot, delicious air. I laugh, all delight.

I hit the water again, spin around, still laughing. I am ecstatic until I recall their hunger, how ferociously they feed.

I swim quickly now, quickly and respectfully, through bodies half the size of my own, toward the outer edge of the school. The two triangular fins at their sides flap gently as they hover. The thin gray veil over their white flesh glistens. They stun with grace and agility. Their eyes hold me. I am lost. I am feed for squid.

One shoots ahead. Now the whole school races. I tumble as they propel above, below, on all sides. I imagine their attack before I feel it, curling into myself, tight, tight. I imagine being ripped flesh. Dead. I am drawn under by the surge of the school as it dives. I struggle to disentangle myself. I taste copper-rich blood. The sea foam is green with it. Their blood, not mine. How? Confusion makes me stupid. A sucker-laden arm encircles my waist. I writhe, but it holds fast. Yet it gives no pressure. In horror I realize it is not attached to the squid. I yank it off and it swims away on its own. I look around, frantic. The water goes ink dark. I swim blindly.

And now the school is gone; the ink gradually clears. The sea horses, the slowest creatures in these waters, are the first things I see. They appear to rise from the ink, like the horse Pegasus, born of Medusa's blood when Perseus cut off her head.

The flash of a sword swings by. I cover my neck with both hands in terror. Who has sent such violence? I search for signs of Rhodope.

The swordfish swings again and again. Fear freezes me. The swordfish flails one last time, with his broad, flat bill. Oh, for a shell to hide in; I am totally exposed. Now the fish swims along contentedly, mouth open, swallowing the drifting pieces of squid head and fin and tentacle.

I let the water lift my arms; I pretend to be dead. With my dark hair fanning out, he may take me for kelp.

He feeds on the dead squid leisurely. At length. Finally he swims away.

I race toward Lemnos, my heart hurting from violent beats. Bright moonlight outlines the rocky shore. I am farther and farther from the swordfish. Slowly, slowly, I let go of the terrible fear. With every breath the warm night air comforts me.

Two different deaths I just escaped. I shudder. I am alive. And, oh, I am grateful for everything.

Is every creature grateful after escaping death? Are the surviving squids celebrating now? I imagine the males depositing packets of sperm in the females with their handlike tentacles in an orgy of relief. The taste of envy fills my mouth: I will never know amorous pleasure. Need stirs within.

I swim out to my rock and sleep fitfully.

The next morning I bask on that rock, still savoring my every breath after the close encounter the night before. A water serpent lifts his venomous head and looks right at me. The serpent hisses and flicks his slender tongue. I think I hear a word, but I cannot make it out. I pull my tail from the water, even though the sea serpent is among the least aggressive creatures.

"Sssssss," he insists, emptying his one lung.

The soft creaminess of his yellow belly looks familiar. This species is not typical of this region of the sea. What is that on the top of his head? A pattern of dots like a star. And, yes, I remember that Hera has a yellow-bellied serpent that does her evil bidding; Zeus' wife is merciless with her enemies. Yet there is no reason for her to wish me harm. "I have done the goddess Hera no ill," I say. "I am no one's enemy."

The serpent slings its wide head from side to side. Another serpent, smaller and without a star, swims up behind. Both lift their heads toward me in double threat.

"You're not looking for me," I say. "I'm not the one." My voice is a prayer.

The smaller serpent leaps and twists away in one

movement, and I see the tail of an oversized cod disappear inside her throat. Now the larger serpent strikes at the cod's head. They consume their prey together, swallowing from both ends at once. When they meet, the larger serpent keeps on consuming, until both the cod and the smaller serpent have disappeared down his throat.

The air is rock silent.

My mouth is open and dry. I breathe hard.

The serpent's body distends sickeningly. The bulges inside him move. He seems to examine me. I cannot speak. Finally he hisses, "Sssssss," and swims off.

The serpent put on that show for my benefit. To tell me always to remember his power. I expect trouble.

SIX

M
A
N

Today I am resting on a large rock offshore. The wind has finally shifted. It blows from the other side of the island. My nose catches the familiar scent before my ears perceive anything. The skin on my arms forms goose bumps. I dive, forcing myself through the thick kelp on the bottom. Finally I stop and wrap the kelp around me. The sea horses I have disturbed fan slowly back to the closest weeds and grab hold with their curling tails. Once they have settled, the bottom looks placid.

How can the sea look placid when there are men on its

surface? My blood pounds in my ears. I am sick with panic.

After a long while I rise to the surface and scan the area.

Six ships have come around the side of Lemnos. They sail in a line, like ducks, toward open sea. They are leaving Lemnos. Have they been here all along? Has the wind kept their noise and smell from me all this time?

Men.

Men whose hot flesh holds secrets. I wither inside from lost hope. These men were here, and I was ignorant.

The ships are leaving.

The men are departing.

Gloom descends. But I fight it. I have already come to terms with my future alone.

I swim past the ships underwater. When I am behind the sixth ship, I surface. A seventh ship is anchored near a sandy beach in a sheltered cove.

My throat thickens with the anticipation of danger. I must not let them see me. I watch, still as a hidden crab.

I know from the light blue color that the water is shallow there, but still deep enough that the ship will not beach. Two men stand on the sand talking with a third, who sits. One man shouts. I strain to hear, but the wind snatches his words. The other man hands the sitting man a bow and a quiver of arrows. I think of lovely Artemis, the goddess of the hunt, who let us touch her silver bow at Thetis' wedding. What will these men hunt?

The sitting man slings the quiver over a shoulder. The three of them argue, their hands flying wildly. Would that I could decipher the words. Now the two men slosh through the water to the ship. The men on board throw ropes for them to climb. The oars move rhythmically. The ship departs.

I watch in disbelief. They abandon the man on the beach. The ways of humans are a mystery. Mermaids would never abandon one of our own. We live as a school; we swim and eat and sleep as a school. My childhood insistence on doing things alone was anathema to my sisters. My choice of living alone now is beyond their understanding. I am sure they believe me dead.

The man gets to his feet. He falls. He struggles to his feet again. I swim closer, careful to keep my head low.

The man staggers, dragging his bow. His quiver of arrows drops. He groans and falls face-first in the sand. Is he ill?

I wait, always hidden. The sun crosses the sky.

The man does not move. Apprehension makes me jumpy.

A large bird alights on the sand beside him. The bird is a scavenger, like our three guardian birds.

My face flashes hot. My eyes burn. I swim fast to the

beach. I pull myself across the sand. The bird flies in alarm.

My hands reach, but I don't know where to touch. A man. I tremble. Then with one swift, determined move, I push the man onto his back. He is but a youth. His mouth is open and full of sand. A stench hits me. He is unconscious, but his chest rises and falls. And his skin is hot. Very hot. Since I have never touched a living man before, I cannot be sure. Yet the rock of fear tumbles in my stomach: I believe he is hotter than he should be. My eyes pass down his body to his legs. His right leg swells below the knee. I sidle through the sand and lean over it. The holes of a serpent bite are red and puffy. The wretched stench comes from those holes. His leg rots. The other men have abandoned him because he has been bitten by a serpent.

This man needs help, and I waited in the water at a distance, mindful only of my own safety. Shame on me.

But, oh yes, the terrifying question must be asked: Is this the work of the serpent sent by Hera? She is the most vengeful of goddesses. Maybe that's why this human's own men abandoned him — for fear of Hera. If I help him, Hera will not forgive me.

I look around. The vulture watches from the brush above the sand line.

I turn back to the youth. He is massive. Fine hair covers his cheeks and chin. But his lips show through, wide and pink. Softly I brush the sand from those lips. I lean over him, my face close and closer. With a sharp intake of breath I realize my urge. I sit up tall again and take his hand in mine. He wears a gold ring with a ruby. His three middle fingers are calloused at the midsection — I glance at his bow and arrows: He must be quite a bowman. I press the fleshy part of his palm, at the base of his thumb. So much of him is like me; so much of him is mystery. And, oh, so much of him is forbidden. I look him up and down. I wonder if his toenails within those thick shoes are long like the toenails of the dead man on Anthemoëssa.

He wears a leather pouch on his belt. I pull from it a half-carved block of wood. From the soft pine emerges the visage of a wide-faced fish with huge eyes and a kind mouth. Her scales are delicate filigree. The man is a skilled whittler. I imagine this fish asleep in a coral reef: blue, purple, green, yellow — a rainbow. I press the carved fish tenderly to my cheek.

I return the wood to the man's pouch with quick resolve. My fingers fly across his wound like insects, buzzing and worried.

If Hera watches, I will pay dearly. If she doesn't, I can, with luck, relieve this man's suffering — this man who admires a rainbow fish enough to carve her image.

I am not a natural healer. I have had neither experience nor need. We of the sea heal on our own, quickly. Or we die. But I know something of healing. I know that land animals lick their wounds. I know that birds pick lice off one another.

I lean over the wound and lick. The slight pressure of my tongue is enough: Pus oozes forth. I roll him heavily toward the water. I press at the edges of the wound and the pus dribbles out. I splash it with salt water and press and splash and press and splash until the milky blood runs ruby red.

The man is still unconscious. What else should I do for him? The men stranded on Anthemoëssa died for lack of fresh water. I pull the man above the water-line, though there is no danger that the tide will rise before I come back. Still, I do it. I will be careful with this fragile man.

I shout to the bird, "Be gone!" I wave my arms violently. The bird flaps away on lazy wings.

I glide into the water and search the bottom. But I am not lucky: There are no turtle shells, no conch shells. I swim to the side of the island where a half-ruined house stands on the beach. I maneuver myself forward, arms then tail fin, arms then tail fin, slowly. The door of the house swings open at a touch. I move through the rubble with difficulty. The sensation of this hard-packed floor on my tail fin is unpleasant. I am clumsy and large and heavy and lost, and I want very much to return to the water. But I remember my mission. This man must live.

I find a large clay bowl, still whole, lined with fragments of ancient flowers. I secure it under one arm. Now my motion is even more hobbled. I leave the house and pass a walled garden. Over the top of the wall I see a tree laden with sunset-colored fruits. Some have fallen in the sandy soil outside. I hold two fruits on my tongue, like Mother Dora held Little Iris' eggs, and I return to the sea with my precious cargo.

I head for the east side of the island, to the mouth of the stream. I pass from the brackish delta up to where the waters run cool and fresh. I scrub the bowl with river sand and fill it with sweet water. Then I balance it on my head and swim back, using the lesson of the bull seal I saw carrying his pup the first time I fled Anthemoëssa.

I set the bowl carefully beside the man. His lips are parted, exactly as they were before. His hand lies with the palm up as if in offering, exactly as I left it. He has not moved. With one finger I touch the very center of his palm; I trace a tiny circle. I tap the ball of each fingertip. Heat rushes to my cheeks and ears.

But my light touch will not save him.

I take the two fruits from my tongue and place them in the fresh water. With my hands I dribble fresh water into the man's mouth. Then I splash more salt water on his wound. His eyelids flutter. He moans. I hurry out into the water and bob in the waves, watching.

SEVEN

H

E

L

P

The man disappeared inland last night. But now he comes onto the beach. I am hiding behind an offshore rock. I fight the urge to swim close. He could harm me if he wanted to.

He carries the water bowl I brought him yesterday. He sets it on the sand and paces.

He limps. I wonder if the pus is back. Will he know to wash it away with the salt water? He calls out, "Hello." He turns around calling, "Hello. Where are you?" He kneels. He pulls on his wispy chin hair. His hands touch the sand gingerly. Now I understand: He examines my tracks. His face is bewildered. He stands up. He looks out to sea and his expression changes to terror. He hunches over and clutches his right calf. After a while he straightens himself and extends both hands heavenward. "Zeus, mighty father, only you can intervene. Help me. Oh, god of all gods, please help me." He turns slowly and disappears into the woods.

I wait. Finally I swim to the beach and look in the bowl. It is empty, but for two fruit pits. Is that all he has eaten? He is a large man, and hunger is cruel.

This island is rich in food for humans. Bird calls make an almost constant background. At dusk I have seen deer. There is fresh water. And there are homes for shelter. He should take better care of himself. But maybe his leg hurts so much, the pain disorients him.

I pull the bowl behind me into the water. I swim around to the stream's mouth and go up against the strong current. I clean the bowl and refill it. Then I bring it back to the beach. The man is nowhere in sight. I leave the bowl and swim to the beach house. I make my way to the walled garden. My tail fin is sore from yesterday's efforts, but my determination is that much greater. The man may survive, and he prays to Zeus. He's a sensible man, a man worth saving.

I cross the rough ground carefully, searching for the easiest path. This time I go through the gate. Bedraggled flower bushes surround a large fountain, full of muddy water and small fish and frogs. I manage to go over to the fruit trees near the wall, though my arms are tiring fast. I hear a stick crack. Is a predator near? I must hurry.

I snatch six fruits from the ground and place them in my mouth. My cheeks bulge like a blowfish. I labor to the sea and bring the fruits back to the man's beach. I leave them in the water in the bowl.

But a human his size cannot live on fruit alone. What did the guests at Thetis' wedding eat besides lamb? Nuts, yes. I swim around the island, looking for the narrow, saw-edged leaves. I come across a grove. The trees are lined up in neat rows. The now extinct people of Lemnos must have planted this grove. I maneuver awkwardly, picking up fallen nuts. I am ever mindful of noises. What will I do if a leopard comes? But leopards don't hunt by day.

I crack nuts, sampling the varieties. I decide on a small round nut with tangy flesh. I could fashion a basket of cordgrass to carry them — but I don't want to take the time. I am anxious to check on the man. My man. I fill my mouth with nuts in their husks and swim back to his beach. The man has not yet returned. I spit out a pile of nuts on the sand beside the bowl.

The meal begins to look interesting. I feel a hint of contentment; this is almost fun. But this meal lacks something crucial. Fish. I cannot pass a day without eating fish. Humans eat fish, too, of course. And other things from the water, like octopus. I think of the strong swimmer who was drowned by the octopus. The swimmer poor Cecilia followed. I won't wrestle an octopus. And now I remember the cavalcade of lobsters on the sea floor not long ago. I enter the water and swim low near the shore. A large spiny male scuttles by himself, a renegade.

I swim farther out, deeper, where the kelp grows tall. I chew at the bottoms of the tough fronds. At last I am rewarded with several strands. I swim back to the lobster. He pokes around an empty horseshoe crab shell as though I weren't there at all. I bunch the kelp and drop it on him, then roll the whole mess, kelp and lobster, into a ball. I bring it back to the man's beach.

I set the lobster-kelp ball on the wet sand and dig a hole until I reach water below. For good measure, I trench a gully to the shoreline. The waves rush up the trench and fill the hole to the brim. I block the gully with sand and drop the lobster-kelp ball into the pool. The lobster thrashes. His tail flaps out of the kelp.

A snapping noise comes from beyond the bushes. I jump, partly from fear, partly from thrill. I roll into the water and swim to the offshore rock.

The man comes onto the beach. His limping is more exaggerated. His shoulders sag. He stops by the bowl and the pile of nuts. He stares at my tracks. He shakes his head again. "What manner of beast you are, I cannot tell," he says loudly. "I fear you." He is silent for a long moment. At last he says, "But you feed me." He leans his head back and shouts, "Where are you?" He holds up his bow and shakes it. "I shot a dove, but I couldn't find where it fell. My arrow went straight through its body and lay wet in the dirt." He puts the bow on the sand. The way he moves, I can tell the bow is heavy. He slips off his quiver and sets it beside the bow. "Help me."

He stands, shoulders squared, waiting.

Finally he kneels. He dips his face in the bowl and drinks water like a deer. He lifts his chin and puts a fruit whole into his mouth. The juice dribbles down the hair on his jaw.

He talks to himself, but in a normal tone now. I cannot catch the words. I want to hear. I miss talk; my sisters always talked a lot. But more than that, I want to know what this man says, what he thinks. I dive and swim underwater halfway to shore. I stick my head out of the water only enough so that my eyes and ears and nose are in the air. If he scans the water carefully, he might see me. But I can swim away in an instant.

A lobster claw emerges over the edge of the pool. Then

the whole lobster climbs out. The man has his back to the pool. The lobster will get away. I go underwater and swim along the bottom. A scallop looks at me with two rows of bright blue eyes. I grab it and it snaps shut. I come to the surface and hurl the scallop. It hits the man in the back of the head.

"Ahi!" The man looks around quickly, one hand rubbing his head. "A lobster. Oh, glorious day." The lobster races to the water. The man lunges, tackles the lobster by the tail.

The angry lobster twists and pinches his hand.

"Ahi!" The man lifts his hand and shakes. "Delicious but infernal, are you?" He shakes harder.

The lobster is flung away. It throws sand in dismay and sets out again for the water.

The man holds his right leg with both hands. He rocks in pain. Then he stands and kicks the lobster toward his pool.

The lobster pinches onto the man's shoe.

"What's this? A clever lobster?" The man limps along with the lobster stuck to his shoe. He goes behind the bushes and bends over. His hands are busy, but I cannot see what he does. He lets out little cries of pain. He limps back onto the beach, still dragging the lobster on his shoe. "And to think I've always called persistence a virtue," the man says with a small laugh. I marvel that he can laugh at this stubborn lobster when he's both hurt and hungry. I want to laugh, too: Man and lobster are ridiculous.

The man's arms are full of sticks. He sets a longer stick aside, then arranges the others into a cone with an open top, like a barnacle shell.

As he kneels, the lobster lets loose of his shoe and hobbles toward the water. The man picks up the kelp ball from the pool and throws it on the ailing lobster. "I'm sorry, valiant warrior. But this may be life or death for both of us." He returns to his cone of sticks. He breaks twigs into a pile, then he pulls two rocks from the pouch on his belt and strikes them together. A spark flies. My breath catches. He strikes again. Another spark. The man puts his face low and blows softly on the twig pile. The sparks jump to the cone of sticks and set them aflame.

I marvel at the glow. I know the story of Prometheus, the Titan who gave fire to humans and endured excruciating torture for his deed. Are the rocks from this man's pouch special, or would any rock do? I have been near open fire twice before. At Thetis' wedding pitfires roasted the lambs. And once lightning struck a tree on the island of Ischia when I sang there with my sisters. The tree was at the water's edge. We listened to the crackle and smelled the smoke and shrank away from the heat.

The flames of the man's fire flicker red and yellow. He

pushes the sticks this way and that, blowing softly. He hums between puffs, as though he has forgotten his pain, but I am sure he has not. He leans to the left, away from that festering right leg, even as he kneels.

A claw peeks from the kelp. Then the rest of the lobster. It moves with difficulty. Yet it still knows the direction of the water.

The man looks over his shoulder at the lame lobster. "One last try, my friend?" His voice is weary and kind. He talks as though he understands the dignity of a creature so low as a lobster.

He picks up the longer stick he has been saving and manages to get to his feet. "I wouldn't kick you this time, even if I still had the strength to do it. You have earned an honorable death." I love the way he talks to this lobster. He limps a few steps, falls. He knocks the lobster over with the stick so that the unprotected line where tail meets abdomen is exposed. He spears it. The lobster curls tightly around the stick. "Worthy foe, I'll bring you the swiftest death I can." The man crawls to the fire and thrusts the lobster into the flame.

The lobster shell whistles, like a muted shriek. A spasm racks the man's chest. He slumps forward. He drops the stick with the lobster into the fire. He collapses.

I do not know if he is still conscious, but he is so close

to the flames, I must take the risk. I come out of the water and move cautiously forward. He moans.

I roll him a body's length from the fire. Then I retreat. He moans still, eyes closed. I'm glad. I don't want him to witness the clumsy way I move on land.

I come around behind him and look at his leg from a distance that keeps me outside his reach. The wound worsens. The swelling is greater, the odor more disgusting.

This serpent bite will not heal.

I remember the serpent show just days ago. I am sure now: Hera has warned me. I should not interfere.

The man moans. He is wracked with pain and hunger.

I am all he has. And in his pouch is a carved parrot fish. This man has a sense of the beauty in the sea. He values it.

I pull the lobster stick from the fire. The shell has turned bright red. I set the lobster on the sand.

I think of the empty horseshoe crab shell that the lobster fiddled with. I go to the water and search the bottom till I find it. I go back to the beach.

The man's leg is hot to the touch. The tight skin around the wound glistens. I break off the horseshoe crab's tail and hold it over the fire until the tip of the tail steams and turns black. It is sharp as an urchin spine. I jab the tip into the center of the wound. The man screams as the pus spurts. His eyes open. His hands clutch at the air. I move back, wincing. Oh, wrong world, that I should have to be the one to bring him this agony.

Pus pours from the wound. I fill the crab shell with seawater and dump the water over the wound and hurry back to the sea. I refill and return and press on the sides of the wound and dump the water, again and again until his blood runs red and the stench ceases.

The whole time, the man hums and rocks his head and shoulders. He crosses his arms at the chest and tucks his hands in his armpits. His eyes stare at nothing. They are dry.

My own eyes drop heavy tears for his pain. He is brave. I remember how he laughed when his struggle with the lobster first began. This man is brave and kind and full of mirth. A miracle man.

The man's rocking subsides. His arms fall free. I quickly move to a safe distance. But his arms stay limp on the sand.

I bring over the pile of nuts. I peel off the husk, crack the shells between two rocks, and set the nutmeats in the horseshoe crab shell. I touch the lobster; it is warm now, no longer hot. I rip out the plump white tail meat and set it on top of the nuts.

The man breathes easily. His eyes are still open. He

blinks at the sky. His eyes do not wander toward me. Yet I am sure he knows where I sit. He knows precisely.

I watch the embers of the fire for a moment. The man stares heavenward. I reach out my hand and push the shell closer to him.

His right hand darts out and touches mine lightly.

I pull my hand back instantly, then roll to the sea and swim away in terror. When I look back, he is looking at me with an open mouth and wonder on his face.

EIGHT

F
I
R
E
&
W
A
T
E
R

The man is gone again. I look at the refuse on the beach: pits and shells. He ate everything, like a messy cub. I look toward the woods. What does the man do when he leaves the beach?

It is early afternoon. The man ate and then slept and then ate again. The sand holds the outline of his body. My fingers hover above it. Before I know what I will do, I am lying in the hollow made by his weight. I wriggle down and his aura envelops me. The strange intimacy almost shocks me. I sit up quickly and move out of the hollow.

The day is bright and warm. There's a breath of autumn, though. The smell. The damp of the air. Demeter, goddess of the harvest wealth, foresees winter. Her beloved daughter Persephone, the radiant maiden of spring and summer, must soon go to the underworld for her annual stay with her husband Hades. Demeter anticipates grief.

I have grieved this whole time on Lemnos. But I don't grieve today. I look at the imprint beside me. The man who made it has seen me. He has touched me. He could have grabbed my wrist and shouted curses. Instead, his touch was gentle. And that gentleness dispersed my grief and opened the way for this strange new feeling — this fear and eagerness that refuse to be teased apart.

All at once, I realize that I've been sitting on the sand lost in thought, as though I were safe. Who knows what might spring from the nearby bushes? I shake with fear and anger at my own carelessness.

I enter the water. This is my home: the sea. I must not forget that. I must stay alert to danger on land.

The man is a land creature.

And, oh, the truth slaps at me like a rough surf: I have allowed myself to take the man's single touch of my hand as a signal that we could know one another. I am stupid and crazy. Hope torments me.

A heron flies overhead, its long orange legs dangling, its wings wide and strong and persistent. Soon the bird is out of sight. I should go, too. I should flee. This island, this man, hold nothing but misery for me.

A billow of smoke rises far off, like a beckoning finger. Obedient, I set my sights and swim underwater straight and fast like a tuna. I swim a long time, letting the motion fill me so that thoughts of the man are held in abeyance.

I surface at last into a hail of hot ash. The seas swell around me. The dark smoke column rises to the clouds. Molten lava pours red and sparkly from the just-born volcanic island's cone top. It is a small island — a minor eruption. A gray rock floats by — the largest piece of pumice I have ever seen. I tap it; it is only mildly warm. I clasp it to my chest with both arms, trying to satisfy a need I refuse to contemplate.

A burning rock splashes in front of me. I duck and swim under the turbulent water and around the island. Where the lava hits the water, boiling bubbles massage me. I twirl. My hair swirls about me. I hold the big pumice rock tightly. The pumice wants to rise so much, I must work to stay underwater.

Another river of lava enters the water, larger and faster than the last one. I swim away, but not fast enough. The tumult washes me aside, bashes me against the sharp edges of the island foundation. I head away and down to cold waters. I am bruised almost everywhere. My tail is singed badly. My whole body buzzes with the sense of danger; a fish needs a healthy tail. My tail is the source of my swimming power.

I float a long while, gathering energy. My eyes dart from here to there, watching for signs of predators. Even the smallest waves bring pain. I have never been so badly injured.

The ashy sky drops its moisture all at once: The rain pounds. I lift my face to the wild downpour and stick out my tongue. I rarely drink fresh water, yet now I greedily drink the sky's bounty. Fire and rain. I think of how Hera cast Hephaestus, the god of fire, out of heaven. For what crime? I am confused from the beating this volcano gave me; I, who have memorized all the tales Amphitrite told us, I remember only part of this tale now. Was Hephaestus banished merely because he was ugly and lame? Oh, shameless Hera. Hephaestus fell to earth — to Lemnos. To the island where the man stumbles with his injured leg.

Hera must hate Lemnos. I remember the serpents. Hera must hate me. I am cursed, like Hephaestus.

I scream. My angry, frightened voice drowns in the waters of heaven and sea. The thick air scratches my throat and burns my eyes. I itch all over, like a snake ready to shed.

But Hephaestus didn't stay on Lemnos; he returned to Olympus. Oh, yes, he escaped Hera's curse, for he married Aphrodite — the goddess Paris called the fairest of all. The only ugly god married the fairest goddess. I have always loved that part of the tale.

Hephaestus now works on Mount Olympus as smith and armorer. He forges weapons. And sometimes his forge is said to be under a volcano. Sometimes it is Hephaestus who causes an eruption.

Has Hephaestus spoken to me today? My damaged tail and battered body make me lame now, like him. And, like him, I want the companionship of someone beautiful. Could Hephaestus be telling me to have hope? To return to Lemnos and see what becomes of this man?

The journey back to Lemnos is slow and difficult. I swim near the surface, ever on watch for predators. I still clutch the pumice. I don't know why. If I were attacked, it would be of no use.

The rain is behind me now. The turgid waters and ashy air, all behind. I swim quickly, gulping fresh air. The sun wanes over Lemnos.

I hide behind my rock, arms clasped around the pumice. The man kneels on the beach over a fire. I gasp at the sight of him. His shoulders are broad and strong. He is handsome, even from a distance. Desire flutters in my stomach. I yearn, against my will, as Hephaestus must have yearned for Aphrodite. The man looks out at the water often. He rotates a skewer with meat. Now he pulls the skewer from the fire and stands it upright, forcing its tip into the land, so that the meat drips onto the sand. He turns to the water and says in a loud voice, "Where are you?" He gestures to the stick of meat. "This time I've prepared you a dinner. Rabbit. Please come be my honored guest." He scans the surface of the water.

I am safely within the shadow of the rock. He cannot lure me with food, like one would lure a simpler animal. His words are cunning, though — I have to admit that. His guest. I shiver. I would love to be his guest, if he meant it truly.

"You're not hungry yet?" He sits down. "I can wait."

I see his right calf better now, but I cannot tell if it is swollen again. I wish he would come into the salt water.

A sharp pinch of pain shoots up from my tail. I look down at the impudent crab. At any other time, such a pinch would be nothing. I'd snatch the crab, crack it open, and suck out the flesh and juices — a little treat. But tonight my poor singed tail aches. I grab fast for this little enemy crab and the pumice floats away, out into the open water.

"Ah. A floating rock. You beckon me into the water?"

The man hesitates. "Do you swear there is no snake nearby?" He rubs his hands in worry. Then he takes off his clothes and lays them in a pile. His body, unlike his face, is not hairy. Except where limbs meet torso. My cheeks grow hot and there is a stirring deep within. He pulls off his shoes. He rubs his bare chest. Then he limps slowly into the water up to his waist. He stops and waits for the waves to carry the pumice to him. When it is an arm's length away, he steps forward, grabs it, and laughs. "Pumice. But this island isn't volcanic. Where did the pumice come from?" He throws himself onto the rock playfully. He bobs for a moment, then the pumice bounces out from under him. He stands up and laughs and throws himself onto the pumice again. It pops out on his other side. He lifts it over his head and shouts, "Play with me."

What a strange thing is this human, that he can be abandoned by his companions with a wound that resists healing, yet he's ready to play at the first provocation. I think again of yesterday, how he laughed at the lobster clinging to his shoe, even as he stumbled on the beach from pain. I lean a little farther out from the rock. I want to see everything, every detail.

The man carries the pumice to the beach and sets it on the sand. "Thank you for the gift," he calls. "I don't know what you want me to do with it. Where I live, women use pumice to soften their skin. Are you saying my skin is too rough?" He scratches his bearded chin. Then he holds his hands in front of his chest and inspects them. "I need my callouses. I cannot shoot the bow without them." He picks up his bow and runs his hands lovingly over it. "Heracles gave me this bow."

I am immediately interested. Heracles was the strongest man on earth. He was born of Zeus and the human woman Alcmene. Hera hated Heracles, of course, as she hates all the children her promiscuous husband fathers with others. She is mean-spirited, like Rhodope; both punish the innocent. Poor Heracles came to a wretched end. But, as far as I could tell, he also deserved it.

"Do you want to know the story of how I got this bow, these arrows?" The man kisses the bow and puts it on the sand. "Come closer and I'll tell you."

The dark deepens, but the fire highlights the man. I see him well. There is nothing to aid him in seeing me, however. I come out from behind the rock and swim close.

"You have to come near. I don't want to shout the tale." The man walks back a few paces, sits on the sand, and waits.

His silence compels, for no mermaid can resist a story.

I swim to the shore as determinedly as I have swum in the past to the storytelling sessions in Mother Dora's grotto.

He sees me and his body jerks to attention.

I stay in the water. I can push off and be under and away in a flash.

His mouth is open. His eyes glow. I see his leg clearly now. The wound looks clean. It heals. The man clears his throat. "There you are. I knew it." He picks up the bow. But the quiver of arrows is out of reach. He cannot shoot me without getting up and going for it. I stay ready to flee. He speaks softly. "Heracles was a great man." He waits as though basking in his pronouncement.

I think back to Amphitrite's many stories about Heracles. I shake my head. It is not normal to interrupt a storytelling session, but the man is so wrong, I must. "Heracles killed his own wife and children in a fit of madness," I say.

"You speak." The man clutches the bow so tightly his knuckles shine white. "Your voice — your voice is marvelous." He licks his bottom lip. He looks awestruck. Then he blinks several times. He stands up.

I swim out.

"No. No, come back. Please." He sits down. "I thought I was talking to myself really. But you understood." He rubs his hands along the wood of the bow. "You spoke." He is silent for a few moments. Then, "We can speak to one another. You and I." His hands go up and down the bow, up and down. "You said something. Yes. You spoke ill of Heracles." He stares into the dark, his face full toward me.

I know he cannot see me. I swim closer, into his sight range once more.

At last, he speaks. "It wasn't Heracles' fault that he killed his family. Hera sent the madness upon him." The man waits. And waits.

I realize with surprise that it is my turn — that's how we will proceed, one then the other. The delight of taking turns in a storytelling session — the delight of sharing the power of the stories — loosens my tongue. I swim into the shallows and choose my point carefully. "He got drunk and made merry in the home of a king whose wife had just died."

"The conversation sharpens into debate." The man's voice is full of amazement. "You are a contentious one. I admire that, though I've never been known for ingenuity at debate." He laughs. "You know much." He shakes his head. "But you don't know enough. Heracles was ignorant of the facts — no one told him the king was a widower."

"He ignored the telltale signs of mourning."

"Heracles never knowingly did a wicked thing in his life."

"All the same, he did a lot of damage."

"The debate loses its charm." The man's voice grows loud. "Heracles went to the underworld and fought Hades himself to bring back that dead queen. He risked his life to make up for his unintended insult. You must not malign his name."

I stay tense. The man is angry. But I can swim out of arrow's reach instantly. Or I could, if my tail were well. I should be careful, I know. Yet my insolent tongue won't stay still. "That he tried to make up for his mistakes doesn't change anything. Heracles was a blundering fool."

"How dare you." The man leans toward me. He opens his mouth to speak, then shuts it. He holds up a finger as if to make a point, then drops his hand. He looks confused. Slowly a smile crosses his lips. He throws back his head and laughs, loud and bellowing. He makes me feel happy and foolish; it is a wonderful laugh. "You're right, of course. Heracles never could do anything without botching it." He pulls on his chin hair. "You are a funny one. People don't speak of Heracles with such disregard. But, then, you aren't a person, are you?"

The question needs no answer.

The man stands up.

I push off into deeper water again.

The man sits down quickly. "Please don't go. I didn't mean to frighten you." He sets the bow on the sand behind him and pushes it with both legs, out of reach of his hands. Then he turns back to me. "I wouldn't hurt you."

I stay where I am.

"To me it doesn't matter what mistakes Heracles made. He was my friend. Almost like a father. When he killed himself, he made me promise to wrap him in the funeral shroud and hold the torch. I lit the pyre that burned him alive, and he lay there quiet, as though on a couch asleep." The man's voice catches; his head drops. "I helped take my best friend's life." He is silent for a long while.

I come onto the wet sand the smallest bit, so that my tail remains in the water.

The man looks up. "Heracles dipped the arrow tips in the blood of the Hydra when he killed her." His voice is soft. I stretch toward him to hear better. "These weapons are the best known to humans. Heracles gave me his bow and these arrows. It was his parting gift. I have pledged to be honorable with the arrows. They stay together, all ten, as a sign of my honor." The man takes deep breaths.

If it is my turn, I yield it. The objections I have to Heracles lose their importance in comparison to the love this man feels for his dead friend.

The man cocks his head. "Heracles stopped on this island once. Did you know that? Did you meet him here?"

I shake my head.

"He came on a ship called the *Argo*. When I am in the woods, I look for signs of him. I half hope that something he left behind will be my means of escape." The man gives a small laugh. "Actually I'd be grateful for even a footprint — anything to make me feel less alone." The man presses his lips together. "But I am not truly alone, am I? You are here." The man opens his hands toward me, then seems to think better of it. He lets his hands fall. "The lobster was good. And hazelnuts are my favorite. And the apricots were the best I've ever tasted." He looks around. "Can I tempt you with rabbit?"

"Does it taste like lamb?"

"Lamb?" The man laughs. "I'd never have expected that question from you."

"Lamb is the only land animal I've ever tasted."

"Did you like it?"

"Oh, yes."

The beautiful man laughs again, and with his laughter my own happiness bubbles up. It would burst from me in song if I didn't stop myself. "Well, rabbit is not as good," he says. "And I'm afraid I've seen no sign of wild sheep. But rabbit is very fine." He walks to the skewer of meat and brings it back. He kneels, not too close, but close enough so that we could touch hands if we stretched. He points at the green needlelike leaves all over the meat. "I wrapped it in wild rosemary. I couldn't find lemons, though. Traditionally it's made with lemons."

The aroma has turned wonderful. My mouth waters. "If you hadn't told me, I wouldn't have known."

He smiles. "But it's fun to tell each other, don't you think? You and I, I wager we have a lot to tell each other." He rips off a chunk of meat and holds it out.

The way he holds it tells much. I could seduce this man with a single song if I wanted. I know that as firmly as I have ever known anything. I could sing and he would forget I was half fish. I could win immortality. Oh, the exquisite award this man unknowingly would give me. We could couple and part. And no one would be harmed. A cost-free prize of eternity.

It is only right that I sing, anyway. For song wells up inside me at the man's words and laugh. At the way he pulls his chin hair. At the incongruence of his physical heft and mild manner. Every little thing about this sensual man evokes song from within. I have been holding that song inside my mouth only with the greatest difficulty.

I open my mouth now, but I remain silent. I cannot let myself sing. Oh, I do not want to, after all. My body goes cold at the notion. And in a flash I hate the idea of singing, for by singing I would seduce this man. I hate the idea savagely. He has not deceived me. I will not deceive him. I am mermaid. I don't want him to forget it. Rhodope can never make me want him to forget it. Rhodope can never make me deny myself.

I come fully out of the water, moving like the monk seal, letting him see how clumsy I am on land. This movement hurts horribly. It is all I can do to keep the pain from showing in my face. I feel the man's eyes travel down my body to my tail, and back again. I fight the urge to slip back into the water, to swim before him, showing off my grace. I look him full in the face, defiant.

His slow inspection is over. He smiles, with no hint of disgust in those eyes.

I take the meat and bite into it. Rabbit is good.

NINE

F
I
S
H

In the night the rains caused by the ash from the distant volcanic eruption arrive at Lemnos. I do not know where the man sleeps. He went inland after dinner. His absence gnaws at me. I wonder if humans are harmed by rain; they seem so frail. I lie on my rock and let the rain wash over my worries.

Only the slightest drizzle remains when the sun's first rays appear. The man seems to come with the sun. He limps onto the beach and cries out, "Help me."

I swim toward him, energized by his voice. The ache

in my tail slows me. The man's bow and quiver, the gifts of Heracles, are over one shoulder. I stop, grateful that my tail kept me from speeding to him. For I am leery again — leery of a man whose honor would be bound up in weapons.

He looks out over the water and sees me. "I was bitten three days ago. I should have died by now. Instead, the wound gets better every time you care for it. Then overnight the poison works its evil again." He shifts his bow and quiver off his shoulder and lays them on the sand. Then he falls on his bottom and stretches both legs out in front. "Please help me."

His posture, his voice, his words, all of them engender trust. And I want so much to help him, to touch him, even if it is only to tend his wound.

I come onto the beach. The smell from his leg turns my stomach. I pick up the horseshoe crab shell. Moving on the land is more difficult than ever — every pace sends stabbing pains up my injured tail. Yet I know it is worse for the man. I go back and forth from the water to the man, pressing out the pus, pouring the water, pressing out the pus, pouring the water. When I am through, the man's eyes are squeezed closed. He breathes hard. I know he fights to keep conscious through the pain. "You have an enemy," I say.

He opens his eyes. "Who?"

"Hera. She sent the serpent." Yes, in a flash I understand all of it. "She hates you because you loved Heracles, the bastard son of Zeus."

The man nods. "That's my conclusion, as well." He shakes his head. "The gods are vindictive."

I press my lips together. "You assume a grave risk to talk like that about the gods."

Then I shake my head at the unwanted memory: "The goddess Dora, the wife of Nereus, says I am daring. But you are worse than me."

"Is that your name, the Daring Mermaid?"

"My name is Sirena." I feel suddenly shy. There is something new and mystifyingly personal about an exchange of names. I fold my hands together, fingers interlaced. "What's your name?" I half whisper.

"Philoctetes. Son of King Poeas."

"Oh." I lower my head. I shouldn't be surprised; after all, I saw his gold ring with the dazzling ruby. "I didn't know you were of royalty."

"On Lemnos what does it matter?"

I nod and lift my head. Philoctetes teases me with a smile. His good nature amazes me. The whole world seems bright and good. I smile back. "Does your leg feel better already?"

"Every time you minister to it, I feel a new strength, as though I really will heal and live."

"Maybe Hera is saving you."

"Torturing me, only to save me?" Philoctetes pulls on his chin hair.

I recognize that as his habit. And I'm so glad to know I'm learning his habits. His chin hair is soft to the touch — I remember. I remember everything about the texture of him.

"I prefer you as a savior," he says jauntily.

I don't know what to answer. I twist my hands in equal embarrassment and fear. I have crossed Hera. A bird walks out from the brush onto the sand. It is a simple golden plover — not a peacock, not the bird sacred to Hera. Yet my fingers still curl around each other like desperate claws. "You should spend as much time as you can in the seawater," I say. "The salt will cure you."

Philoctetes purses his lips. "The serpent could bite again."

"I doubt it. Hera thinks you're dead by now. The serpent has returned to wherever he came from."

Philoctetes chews on his bottom lip. "Unless Hera is watching."

"She's not."

He looks at me in astonishment. "How do you know?"

"There's a war going on." I speak with empty bravado, but the man does not know that. I throw my hair over my shoulder and act unconcerned. "All the gods are involved in the war."

"I know about the war. I was on my way to fight at Troy for the glory of the Greeks. My fleet stopped here to fill up on fresh water, but then I got bitten by the serpent. . . . "

"And your men abandoned you."

"Yes." Philoctetes' voice betrays deep anger.

"People are not loyal."

"Not all of them."

I think of how Philoctetes was loyal to Heracles to the very end. He deserved better treatment from his own men. I move toward the water. "Come." I wince.

"Are you hurt?"

I shake my head.

"Yes, you are. Your tail hurts."

"Not badly."

"And you have welts and scratches on your shoulders and back. I can see them now, in the light of day."

I go into the water. "Come into the sea and get well."

Philoctetes knits his brow. Then he smiles and points behind me. "Look."

I turn. The sun shines brightly through the mist and a wide rainbow crosses the sky. Hope swells within me. Perhaps Hera is truly absent. I turn back to Philoctetes. "It is a good omen."

He undresses and stands. "I like to stay near the shore." He hesitates. "And I don't like to be touched in the water, all right? No playing around."

I think of him jumping on the pumice yesterday. He played in the water then.

"No dunking." He clears his throat. "No splashing, either."

Suddenly I understand. "You don't know how to swim, do you?"

Philoctetes lifts his chin. "It's not a laughing matter."

"I wasn't about to laugh." I think of the men who perished on Anthemoëssa. "I won't let you drown."

Philoctetes doesn't look completely reassured. He walks into the sea as if marching into battle. He stops when the water hits his waist.

"You'll have to come deeper if you want to learn to swim."

"Who said I wanted to learn to swim?"

"Suit yourself." I swim out, but not too far. My tail has

made me vulnerable to attack. I keep on the alert. I dive. The sea is rich and thick today, like the petals of the roses scattered at Thetis' wedding. The volcanic ash has been washed by the underwater currents so that it reaches even here. It forms a film over the sea bottom. I swim low, back toward the man. A bed of scallops winks at me. Only yesterday I hit the man in the back of the head with the scallop. Only yesterday he battled with the lobster. I smile at the memory. I make a nest of my hair and fill it with scallops. Then I swim along until I see Philoctetes' nakedness in front of me.

This is man. He stands in the water oblivious of my eyes. He showed no hesitation when he undressed before. And he was naked last night as we ate — with no sign of that modesty Mother Dora once explained to the mermaids. Maybe I was mistaken. Maybe I could not seduce Philoctetes if I tried.

Maybe I am not female to him.

My throat tightens.

But it doesn't matter if he wants me. We are getting acquainted. We are making friends.

And friends are to play with. That's what Philoctetes would want — I know that much about him already. He'd want to play. And a mermaid alone, separate from her school, needs a playmate desperately. I swim a circle around Philoctetes' legs. Is it too cruel a joke? I cannot help it; I'm giddy. I nibble at his toes.

"Ahi!" Philoctetes runs for the beach. "Help!" He throws himself on the sand.

I come halfway up on the sand, laughing. I dump the scallops on his upturned feet.

Philoctetes rolls over. He is covered with sand. "You are wily." His voice accuses, but his eyes dance with glee.

I can't stop laughing.

Philoctetes looks at the scallops. "A peace offering, is that it?"

"A breakfast."

He sighs loudly. "Are you always capricious?"

"You should rinse off."

Philoctetes dips his body in the sea. Then he collects sticks and builds his cone.

"Are they special rocks?"

Philoctetes looks at me and pauses. He goes to his pile of clothes and dries his hands. He brings his shirt to me and reaches for my hand. The very idea is like a jolt of lightning. I pull back against all my wishes. He swallows and I see the lump of his throat move up and down. His neck is slender like mine. I realize I offended him by moving away. He thinks I'm still afraid of him. And I am — but not the way he thinks. I feel unsure of what to do. I try to smile.

He nods and tosses me his shirt. "Dry your hands." I pat my hands with the shirt. Philoctetes reaches into his pouch and finds the rocks. He extends his hand and looks at me steadily. I open mine. He drops the rocks into my hands. "Flint. Strike them together as hard as you can."

The precious fire rocks are hard, like any other rock. Gray, like any other rock. But I feel their specialness. I bend over the cone of sticks.

"Wait." The man crumples a few sticks into dusty twigs. "Let me get the tinder ready."

I strike once. Nothing. I strike harder. A spark flies and instantly goes out. I strike a third time and as the spark touches the tinder, I blow.

"Who taught you to blow on sparks?"

"I watched you when you cooked the lobster."

"You're quick." He smiles. "But I knew that already."

His praise makes me want to swim and dive and play tag. I squirm and strike the flint and blow again. The tinder flares. I drop the flint and blow continuously. The flame leaps to the cone of sticks. I sit up tall and clap in pleasure.

Philoctetes laughs and drops onto the sand beside me. "Your first fire is a complete success."

"How did you know it's my first?"

Philoctetes laughs harder. "Oh, sweet Sirena." He puts

his hands behind him and leans back on stiff arms. "I could watch you build a fire every day for the rest of my life and never tire of it. I cherish the joy and satisfaction in your eyes."

The word *cherish* repeats in my head. I feel almost dizzy.

"You appreciate Prometheus' gift. The god would be gratified to know he's your hero." Philoctetes gazes at me and his expression grows thoughtful. He holds up his finger. "You, Sirena, you who spoke so harshly of Heracles, did you know that it was Heracles himself who freed Prometheus? Zeus had bound Prometheus with chain to a rock and a vicious eagle ate his liver every day. At night his liver grew back — and each day the eagle returned. Prometheus knew unlimited agony, all because he gave humans the gift of fire against Zeus' express wish." Philoctetes' voice rises high and strong, then plummets. His cheeks grow ruddy. His eyes shine wet.

I, too, want to cry for Prometheus. I, too, rage against Zeus. Oh, Philoctetes is the best storyteller I have ever heard. I hang on his words.

"But Heracles freed him." Triumph beats through his words. "Not many would risk the wrath of Zeus."

"Not many would dare befriend one who did." I look him full in the face. "You are as brave as Heracles, but I hope you are smarter."

Philoctetes laughs again, a laugh of surprise and delight. Then his face turns sober. "Not many would dare befriend a man cursed by Hera." His hand reaches out, steady and firm. He touches my tail. This time I do not pull back. I cannot move — whether from fear or hope, I do not know. He runs his hand lightly over my scales, from belly to tail fins. I am afire. I could scream with this delicious pain. His finger traces the outline of my fins. As it passes over the singed parts, he says softly, "This is where it hurts." He points at my shoulder. "Those bruises must hurt, too."

Need washes me, scours me raw. I long for his hand to move again, to touch me again. Not just my fish half, but all of me.

His eyes take me in, tail to head. They caress me. His hand moves just the slightest bit toward my shoulder. Then he lets it fall on the sand. He looks away.

I want to see his eyes. I want to know what he feels. And, oh, I want so much to sing. My song should enter this man just as his story entered me. My melody should bring his flesh to a frenzy of desire. My mouth is partway open already. I remind myself of my vow not to seduce him. I tell myself no. But it is so hard to keep silent. So hard.

Philoctetes clears his throat. "After breakfast, if it doesn't hurt you too much, will you teach me to swim?"

He looks at me, and his eyes now show nothing. Or maybe, maybe, there's the slightest hint of sadness.

I am confused. He has changed the direction we were moving in. Has my tail repulsed him, after all? It would take so little to overcome that repulsion. One song. Oh, my evil thought. Where is my resolve to be mermaid, apparent to all eyes, proud and free? Where is my honor? I must fight harder against the curse of Rhodope. I nod, trying to make my eyes as unrevealing as this man's.

We eat scallops in silence. A cooked scallop is oddly palatable. I study the low bushes beyond us. I focus on the color of the leaves. I force carnal thought of the man from my mind. He is an animal of another species. Nothing more. He touched me out of curiosity. Nothing more. The leaves are as white-green as the salty sea south of Crete.

"Ready?" Philoctetes rises and walks into the water.

The lesson begins. I throw myself into it with every bit of energy I have. He is a quick study, but his fear of the water is his enemy. He paddles along, feet off the bottom, slopping in the sea like the land animal he is. Though I assure him I won't let him drown, he refuses to venture from the shallows. We work half the day. Eventually he is hungry once more. He leaves the water, takes his bow and quiver, and disappears into the trees.

I pass the rest of the day swimming and eating. That evening Philoctetes and I share clams and abalone, my contribution, and roots and rabbit, his contribution. We tell stories late into the night, drinking warm water out of a two-handled earthenware amphora Philoctetes found in one of the dilapidated houses. He rubs the fat belly of the jug as he talks animatedly. My eyelids droop. Finally he tires as well. He goes inland to sleep and I return to my rock offshore.

He is right about his wound. For in the morning he stumbles down to the beach in agony and I tend to his festering leg. Then it is as though his leg is cured: He is full of energy once more and we immediately get to work on swimming. But to little avail; he cannot stay underwater for more than a matter of a few minutes. And his skin is delicate. He needs to hike to the fresh stream and rinse off the sea salt after our lessons. But the biggest problem is that he has no grace. I show him a simple glide and he flops and curls like a dying octopus.

The next few days pass in this routine: I treat his wound, we have a futile swimming lesson, we eat. Then he goes inland for much of the day and I explore the surroundings of Lemnos. We meet for dinner and stories. He shows me what new treasure he has unearthed in his scavengings in the human houses. Many of the things he finds have been destroyed, as though someone purposely broke everything of value. He bemoans this state of affairs, but he is persistent in his search. He has a shovel now, and he seems pleased with this tool. And he has a small knife for whittling. He crafts little animals with that knife as he tells stories about the heroes he loves — mostly about Heracles. Then we part, to sleep.

Each night I struggle to hold in my songs, and each night I win by a slight margin. We become friends, this man and I, though I have noticed that he seems to look at me less and less. Perhaps the sight of me distresses him. Perhaps he is my friend against his own impulses. Sometimes I think he sneaks a glimpse of me, but when I turn to him, he looks away, as though embarrassed for me — for my fish half.

Still, we are friends, fast and close. We merge in storytelling.

But neither of us is content. He comes to me exhausted from his searchings for human objects in the houses. And I am no better off. His lack of progress in swimming frustrates me.

One day while Philoctetes is inland, I flip over and over in the water and think about his problems in swimming. I am successful in helping him with his arms, for I, too, have arms, though I rarely use them in swimming unless I want to rise or dive or change direction. But his legs are the puzzle. He moves them like he's running, and running doesn't make sense in the sea. How do creatures with legs swim?

Frogs. There are no frogs in the sea, of course. But there are plenty of frogs in the freshwater fountain in the garden of the beach house. I go there now, my chest tight with optimism. I make my way through the gate and to the fountain. My singed tail hurts a little still, so I go slowly. The fountain overflows from rain the night before. The frogs are active and happy. They are so funny, I laugh. They shoot out their powerful back legs, then bend them and shoot out again.

I understand now. Yes. I will teach Philoctetes to swim like the most competent of frogs.

Crack!

I turn. A brown bear wanders in through the gate. My hands grab at the stone wall of the fountain I sit on. I look at the side door of the house. It is so far, and I move so poorly on land. There is no chance I could get there before the bear. My tail curls backward instinctively.

The bear looks at me. Her nose twitches. She comes forward a few steps, paws squishing in the puddles of rainwater, fallen branches cracking under her weight. I have seen bears fish in shallow waters. None has ever come after a mermaid, so far as I know. My hands hold so tight, the stone of the wall cuts into them. The bear comes closer. She is full grown, I am sure. She lifts her upper lip to reveal sharp white teeth. She growls. The sound fills my head, would split my eardrums.

"Listen, Orsa," I say. "Listen to me. We are friends."

The bear throws her head back. She growls louder. She stretches her muzzle forward and takes a deep whiff.

"I smell like fish," I say, "but I taste awful. You would hate me."

She comes forward and lets out a screaming growl that makes my blood run icy.

I turn my face to the sky and open my mouth to the only weapon I know. My song comes high and keening:

> Orsa wild, have pity on me
> Spare this child of the sea
> Eat the luscious apricot
> Then take your leave, tarry not

The bear pauses, her muzzle lifted. Her eyes glaze over. She seems to totter, as though she may lose her balance altogether. Then her nose twitches again. I see myself in her glassy eyes: I see fish.

I sing with my heart in my mouth:

Orsa wild . . .

The arrow flies. It barely grazes the bear's nose. She cries out in alarm.

"Be off!" Philoctetes jumps down from the garden wall. "Be off, before you force me to slay you."

The bear turns and lumbers out the garden gate and away.

I collapse, slipping from the lip of the fountain wall, my back pressed against the side stones. I cross my arms over my chest and try to catch my breath.

Philoctetes fetches his arrow and carefully puts it with the other nine in his quiver. He moves as though he's in a dream — slowly, much, much too slowly. He kneels by my side. "Sirena? She's gone, Sirena. She won't come back." He looks around. "What were you doing here? Getting me more fruit? You shouldn't do that. You shouldn't come so far onto the land. Anything could kill you." He tugs at my arms and takes my hands into his. "If I hadn't been rummaging around in the house across the way . . . Oh, Sirena, you must never come out on land this far again. Promise me, beautiful Sirena."

I look at him, half dazed. He has called me beautiful. "She wanted to eat me."

Philoctetes tightens his hands around mine. "I heard your song. It entered my heart like nothing ever has before."

He hears my song in his head. He's not listening to my words. Cursed song that beguiles and bewitches. His face fills with love. Oh, how much I wanted that love. But not this way. I look into Philoctetes' eyes and see a beautiful young woman. I remember myself in the bear's eyes. They are two different reflections. Philoctetes cannot see the me that I am, that I must be. I am crying. "Bear eat fish. Do you hear me, Man?"

Philoctetes looks at my tail. Then he touches my face; his finger draws circles in my tears. "We are all made of little pieces. We are all part this and part that. We are air and water and fire and dirt. But you, Sirena, you are more. You are fish and more."

"What more?" I ask in desperation.

"Ah, much more. For you are also Sirena." Philoctetes leans forward and his lips meet mine.

I think perhaps, oh terrible thought, I hear far-off laughter. Is this the laughter of Rhodope, who harbors so much hatred she rejoices at this error?

But Philoctetes' kiss is perfect. And I am not responsible for this mistake. I cannot change what is. I could not disabuse an enchanted man, even if I tried. I cannot undo what a nymph has done.

Philoctetes' brown chest is against mine. He kisses me on the neck. He nuzzles my ear. And I am moaning and kissing him back. I circle my arms around him and accept the sweet mercy of passion.

The Years

PART III

TEN

I
m
m
O
R
T
A
L
I
T
Y

I wake to stars. Philoctetes, beside me, breathes shallow in peaceful sleep. I listen for what woke me, but I hear no slip of serpent through water. No rustle of peacock feathers. Nothing that hints of threat — of Hera. I am simply awake. Utterly untired. I move carefully away from the warm halo of Philoctetes' body to the water. I expect my tail where I burned it to hurt a bit still, my shoulders and ribs to ache a little. I expect my fingers and palms to be raw from digging into the stone of the fountain wall. Instead, I feel strong and ready. My tail has finally healed.

My bruises have disappeared. My hands are surprisingly without blemish. It is fitting — for my body is a vessel filled with delight. I am married, at last.

I ease into the water and swim around the cove aimlessly. I turn onto my back and float. The air carries odors I recognize, but they are different tonight. They come to me individually; my nose picks out heady oleander, the rotted droppings of a distant leopard, the rich maturity of plums. The air yields noises, too, and again my ears pick each one out from the others: the whisper jump of a predatory spider, the heartbeat of a dove, the light snore that comes now from my man. Each smell, each tiny sound, has integrity and strength. My sensations are different tonight. Is this the difference between those who have loved and those who haven't? The sky glitters with distant fires. I feel I could fly to them if I tried. But I have no wish to leave this cove — no wish to leave Philoctetes. Ever.

Love is a miracle.

Lovemaking is a miracle.

Philoctetes is a miracle.

I curve backward and dive. I roll along the bottom of the sea. I twist in and out of the kelp bed. I slither along the rocks to where it gets shallow, closer to the sleeping man that I now know as mate. I swim faster as I approach him. My pulse quickens. My lips tingle. I swim so fast my sight blurs. I cannot wait to be with him again. Oh, my lucky heart.

Ahi! My shoulder rips open. I back away from the mussel-covered rock I collided with and surface quickly through the blood that makes the salt of the sea stronger than ever. Savage pain explodes through my body. The exposed bone shines white in the moonlight. Nausea rises in my throat. My head clouds. I know I am about to swoon, about to drown.

But even as I watch, the flesh heals over the bone, leaving no trace of the gash. Not one more drop of blood. I stare, dumbfounded.

All pain has vanished.

Oh, it has happened!

I am immortal.

The knowledge makes me giddy. I am tempted to tease a shark. To bait the she-bear. To seek out a swordfish. Is it really true? But how could it not be? The decree of the gods is final.

I am happy. Somewhere in me I know I should not be so cleanly happy, when I am living out a curse put upon me by Rhodope. But in this moment nothing seems evil.

I swim to the beach and curl up against Philoctetes.

He wraps his dry body around my wet one without waking. I am impatient for him to waken. But I can wait. I have time.

Immortality and Philoctetes.

Immortality and love. What more could I ask for?

ELEVEN

SWIMMING

We swim through the kelp. We chase each other and play hide-and-seek. We rest again on a rock.

Philoctetes moves a finger into a lock of my hair and draws circles until he is caught fast. He pulls me gently toward him; our lips touch, linger. Then he carefully frees his finger, stretches his arms into the air, and flexes them. "I want to swim better."

"In these last few weeks you've become a marvelous swimmer. Probably the best human swimmer alive."

"I want to swim as fast as you."

"Don't be silly."

He puts a pretend pout on his face. "I want to swim faster than you."

"I'm half fish, Philoctetes."

"Then I want to be an honorary fish. Look." Philoctetes points to the flash of silver. "Tunas." He dives after them.

I catch up as he surfaces.

He looks around in surprise. "They're gone."

I laugh. "Not even another fish could outswim a tuna. You didn't stand a chance."

Philoctetes purses his lips. "Hmmm. I wager there's a fish that I could outswim." His brow furrows. This matters to him. I am glad: My mate wants to master the sea.

"Come," I say.

We swim around the island, resting on rocks. The day is hot. I scan the surface of the water. And, yes, I finally spy them. I point.

Philoctetes looks. "Jellyfish. Do you mock me? Saying the only fish I can swim faster than are floaters?" He pinches my side playfully.

"Even a jelly can propel itself quickly when it wants to. But that wasn't what I meant. Follow me." I go straight for the cluster of blue-pink bobbing bubbles. "Stay behind me."

I hear Philoctetes' arms cut the water at my rear. I hear his breath. And now I hear the loud slurp I hoped for.

"What was that?" Philoctetes grabs my arm.

"See?" I point at the sunfish. It is almost double my length: This one belongs out in Oceanus' waters.

"Ahi!" Philoctetes swims quickly for the closest rock.

"Wait."

"He's huge," Philoctetes calls over his shoulder.

"But harmless. He eats only jellyfish."

Philoctetes reaches the rock. He holds on, breathing hard. "He's a noisy eater."

"So are you."

Philoctetes blinks. Then he laughs.

"I believe you can outswim him."

Philoctetes wipes the water from his brow. "How do I engage him in a race?"

"Pull his tail. Only don't get stung by the jellyfish."

Philoctetes swims toward the shy sunfish, who takes off out to sea. A little later my mate is at my side. "Very funny. The sunfish has no tail."

"But you had to overtake him to find out." I smile.

Philoctetes smiles back. He slings his head sideways to get the hair out of his eyes. "You come with me now." He kicks up a wake as he swims to a high rock. He scrambles to the top. "Watch." His voice carries the outrageous pride of a youngster. "Watch me." He leaps and somersaults in the air before hitting the water.

I clap as he comes up for breath.

He swims over beside me. "Want a contest?" His eyes sparkle with the tease. No matter how well he swims, I will always be able to swim faster and longer and deeper. But he can make fancy dives from the rock, something I'll never be able to do.

And now it's my turn to pinch him. "You have already won."

He crows gleefully, and I laugh.

TWELVE

T
H
E

B
O
A
T

I build the fire expertly. Philoctetes watches, half awake, half asleep. I have been to the fecund marsh on the other side of the island. I spied a nest in the cordgrass there yesterday and this morning I stole four eggs. They will delight Philoctetes. Eating seems to be his favorite pleasure — or second favorite.

He rolls over and over on the sand until he lands with a thud against my back. His hand snakes around to my belly and strokes.

I turn and lie beside him in the cradle of his arm. "There's something baking in the earth under the fire."

"Ah." Philoctetes smiles. "Let me guess. Eel?"

"Something round."

"Turtle eggs."

I shake my head. "Nothing from the sea."

"From the land?"

"The air."

"Bird eggs?" Philoctetes sits up. "Really?"

"A marsh bird was silly enough to lead me to her nest."

"Thank the gods for the silliness of birds." He rubs his hands together in anticipation. "Will they be ready soon?"

"I just built the fire."

"So there's time for a story." Philoctetes gets up and goes to his wooden chest, dug halfway into the ground among the bushes. He takes out a long skinny strip of deer hide and a chalice full of bear fat. He comes back, bends his knees, and crosses his ankles. Then he dips the fingers of both hands into the bear fat and works the hide thong.

I wiggle to a comfortable position in the sand, getting ready for this favorite of rituals: the storytelling.

He leans toward me. His hands work continually on that leather. "Would you like to know the story of how Heracles saved Theseus from Hades?"

"You mean when he pulled Theseus from the Chair of Forgetfulness?"

"Oh, you know it."

"You told me."

Philoctetes smiles ruefully. "I'm the one who grows forgetful. Have I exhausted all my tales of glory and honor in just these few months?"

I marvel at how any creature can survive with such a poor inner clock. "It's almost exactly a year."

"A year?" Philoctetes' voice becomes soft. His face is thoughtful. "Time races."

I think of Father Time. I have never heard a tale of Cronus' doings. I sit up and press my cheek against Philoctetes'. He looks gloomy. I whisper encouragement. "Then Time carries us on his shoulders."

Philoctetes wraps the first section of thong around one forearm. It bends easily; he has made it supple. He massages fat into the next section. "Time leaves me behind."

"Do you miss humans?" My voice is clear; it doesn't betray my shaking heart.

Philoctetes stays silent a long while. Then he leans toward me. "I walk along the paths they built here and I think of the busy streets at home, with fountains at the crossroads. And sometimes I sit in the amphitheater they built into the slope of a hill and I imagine the theater that must have gone on. I wager that with this small a town, they played a lot of bawdy farces about their daily life."

"Bawdy? Why bawdy?"

"The public tavern walls are covered with erotic paintings, and there's even a tiny brothel behind it, with two beds in cubicles off a hall. Probably for visiting sailors, but certainly some of the locals had trysts there. Maybe that's why the women killed their husbands — jealous rage."

"And this is what you miss?" My eyes sting. I blink.

"No, oh, no." He loops the leather thong around my shoulders and draws me close. "That's exactly my point. I think about the life the people of this island had when it was thriving, before the women rebelled, and I don't miss it one bit." He lowers his head. "It's not those things I miss. It's the rest of it. All the things men are off doing."

"What things?"

"Traveling the seas . . ."

"You travel the seas. You swim perfectly."

"I go nowhere when I swim." Philoctetes looks away. "How the women of this island got along without boats I cannot fathom."

"Boats?" I go numb.

"They must have destroyed them purposely, or I'd have found old ones." Suddenly he lets go of one end of the thong, so that I am free. He unwinds the end of the thong from his arm, gets up, and puts the leather and the bear fat back in the wooden chest. He returns and sinks down near me, tugging at the tips of his beard. "It'll be spring soon. As you said, almost a year has passed. It'll be good sailing weather."

My head is empty; I dare not think, for I know if I do, this conversation will hurt more than I can bear. I repeat his words slowly: "Sailing weather."

Philoctetes looks at me as though trying to make up his mind. "I haven't told you, but I'm building a sailboat."

"A sailboat."

"Yes."

"The waters here are choppy more often than not — much more dangerous than the waters near Anthemoëssa."

Philoctetes nods. "That's why it's taking so long. I had to design it carefully." Enthusiasm strengthens his voice. He stands. "Want to see?"

"Yes," I say, half to myself.

Philoctetes sets out running along the shore toward the marshland, all thoughts of the baking eggs lost. I follow in the water, unthinking. Then he splashes his way into the marsh, thwacking the cordgrasses aside with the back of his arm.

And there it is. The boat has two pine logs for a base.

Short wooden planks are strapped across them with leather thong, all forming a platform the length of Philoctetes' body.

I'm amazed. He's been building this boat and I didn't even know it. The cordgrasses hid it well.

"These came from tables," Philoctetes is saying, pointing to the planks. "And look." He cups his hands and fills them with water. Then he pours the water onto the platform of the boat. It spreads out in a puddle along a joint. "I crushed shells and mixed them with pine resin, and it made a good plug between the boards. No water can pass."

"And a sail?"

"I've prepared a small pile of deer hides. I pounded them thin."

"Oh." I am so stupid. Philoctetes sat before me day after day, month after month, making leather thongs and it never occurred to me to ask why. And when he wasn't with me, he was off somewhere pounding hides thin for sails. My husband works on a means to leave Lemnos. To leave me. I remember the doomed men on Anthemoëssa and how they searched for wreckage. They needed a ship for survival. But Philoctetes can survive on Lemnos very well. It is not survival that urges him on.

"I thought you might laugh at me," he goes on. "But, really, it could work. With a little luck. I have to try."

"It'll work," I say slowly, almost against my will.

Philoctetes grins. "You think so? Will you help me finish it?" He glows like a little boy again.

I bite my tongue. Can't he see how I feel?

He examines the plug between the planks, murmuring to himself about where he needs to add more. I swim off, to deep waters.

We spend the next weeks moving in and out of the cordgrass, disturbing the fiddler crabs, who brandish their colorful outsized claws in warning. I am unsure how distant the closest inhabited land is, but I know it's far. And this boat is bound to be unwieldy, so it will travel slowly. Worry weighs my hands. But I sew the sail in silence as Philoctetes mounts the mast and attaches low sides to the platform. And when I am tempted to speak, I turn my attention to the black snails that feed on the algae covering the cordgrass, to the clam worms as big as small snakes that feed on dead razor clams, to the ribbed mussels that poke halfway out of the mud. Their simple lives almost soothe me.

Now and then I stuff my ears with marsh mud, for I think I hear far-off laughter — nymph laughter — Rhodope's laughter.

The boat seems ready many times. Philoctetes climbs aboard and we set out with me in the water, leading. But he always finds some flaw in the crafting that makes us return.

I say nothing as Philoctetes reviews each failure and adjusts the sails, the rudder. I want to ask what will happen if he succeeds. I want to know his intentions. But his answer could destroy me. I am not ready to hear it. Perhaps I will never be ready.

And I can no longer bear to help him. I find other tasks that fill my time whenever he calls for my aid. He can perfect his cursèd boat alone.

Finally the boat passes Philoctetes' test, going around Lemnos. We set out immediately for the long trip. We head west. I tell Philoctetes that the closest islands are east. I point out that, should we need to stop, we risk much going west. He responds that the Greek mainland lies west.

It is close to evening on the second day. Philoctetes lets loose the sail. Its end flaps in the quiet breeze. He rests against the side of the boat. "Come in, Sirena."

I am disturbed by his request. I don't want to rush returning him to civilization, of course. But I don't want him in the middle of the sea any longer than is necessary. We should travel for as long each day as he can stand. "It can't be time to sleep yet."

"I need you now." He reaches out his hands. They are

raw from maneuvering the thongs of the sails. I can see from the way he moves his shoulders how weary he is.

My energy is infinite, but his isn't. I give him my hands and he pulls me in without a groan, though I know he aches everywhere. And now I see that his supply of fresh water is more than half gone. On Lemnos I never had occasion to think about the quantity of water he needs daily. Danger prickles my cheeks. "The fresh water lowers —"

"Hush." Philoctetes puts his arms around me. "We're close to land. I can feel it."

I shake my head. I've lived with Philoctetes long enough to know that humans can't sense much in the world around them; it is bald hope that speaks.

"Sirena."

"I'm listening."

"Something plagues my mind."

"Speak, Philoctetes."

"You are immortal, my love, but I grow older day by day." He holds me tighter. "There will come a time when you won't want to be with me."

"Never."

"I will weaken, Sirena. I will bend with age."

"I don't care."

"You will, Sirena. What do you know of aging? You've

told me of your life before you met me. You knew immortals. And you knew fish. Neither of them grow old. Immortals stay the same always. And fish get eaten as soon as they start to slow down."

I pull away from him and sit so that we face each other. Even in the dark, I can see the shine of his eyes. This is the moment I've been longing for and dreading: the revelation. I know instantly where this leads: He intends to leave me when we get to Greece. He wants to convince me that it's better for both of us. He believes it, I know. He believes I will fall out of love with him. This is why he built the boat. This is the most important reason. All at once I forgive him for building it, and my love for him is stronger than ever. "I will love you always, Philoctetes."

"Oh, Sirena. There's so much to it. You don't understand. But I'm tired now. I can hardly think. Please, put your head on my shoulder again. We can talk tomorrow."

I want to argue more. I shake my head. But he doesn't see me; he sleeps already, the deadened sleep of the exhausted.

Oh. I know our separation would never be better for me. But, oh, is it possible? Could leaving me be better for him? Would it pain him to grow old when I don't? I stare into the night, hoping an answer will come.

In the corner of the boat where he has secured his

bow and arrows and the oars that he brought along for extra safety, I spy a small box. I didn't notice it before. I stretch out my hand, but it is impossible to reach without disturbing Philoctetes. I maneuver the tip of my tail fin so that I can brush it. It is smooth on the sides. But the top is made of uneven tiny squares. A metal latch shines gold in the new moonlight. My tail fin is not agile like fingers, nor am I sure that I have the right to open this box even if I could. I rub my fin along the sides in wonder. Philoctetes did not have this box when his men left him on Lemnos, of that I am sure. So he found it on the island. That in itself isn't odd. But why didn't he show it to me? He shows me the tools he finds, the pots and pans. He describes to me the furniture. But he never even spoke of this box, yet it mattered enough to take it on this journey: He counts it among the essentials. My tail fin fiddles with the latch.

Splat! We are showered with spray. Three huge black giants fly above us. In an instant I understand: manta rays. Their fins flap like wings. If I had been in the water still, I'd have known they were coming from the rush of fish before them. I could have pulled us out of their path. As it is, the strange wood of the boat gives me no information about the sea world below. The rays hit the water with a boom like thunder. We are thrown high.

Splash!

Alone in the water.

I find Philoctetes easily, and thank everything good and holy that he is a strong swimmer. We locate the boat and right it. The mast has broken clear off. I realize that if it hadn't, we might not have been able to turn the boat upright again. Still, the loss frightens us — so much so that neither of us speaks. Philoctetes climbs in. Suddenly he spins around and dives back out.

I follow, confused.

He comes up with a gasp of woe.

"What is it, Philoctetes? You must get back in the boat."

"An arrow is missing. I tied the quiver down. I stuffed cloth in the top. But one shook free." Urgency thins his voice. He dives again.

I dive with him.

The sea is brown here. Even with my vision so sharpened by immortality, I cannot see but an arm's length below the surface. I rise for breath.

Philoctetes pants beside me.

"You won't find it in the dark. And there could be more rays. Please, Philoctetes, get in the boat. Let me search."

"They are my responsibility."

"On the sea you are my responsibility. I know the arrow is precious to you, Philoctetes. Let me find it."

Philoctetes' sigh ends as a groan. He swims to the boat.

The water is eerily calm after the disturbance of the rays. That's good — it means the waters themselves haven't worked to steal the arrow. I dive deep, deeper than I think the arrow, with its large fine feathers, could possibly have sunk by now. I swim in a wide circle, flailing my arms blindly. I come up for breath. Philoctetes hangs over the side of the boat but he says nothing. I dive again and swim in ever smaller circles until I am under the boat again. Then I begin once more in the large circle, but this time I dive a little less deep. Each time I come up for breath, I hear Philoctetes swallow, but he asks nothing. I search. My hands meet no wood, no feathers. I am thorough. But anything could have happened to that arrow. The rays could have broken it as they came crashing into the sea. They could have sucked it down with them as they dove.

I swim and search and breathe and dive and circle and search. I remember Philoctetes' words when he first showed me his arrows — he keeps them together as a sign of his honor. All his stories are about honor. It is what keeps his soul alive — more than my love for him. Oh, wretched lost arrow.

I am close to the top now. I see shadows at this level. What? My hand closes over the shaft. I go weak with relief.

I swim to the boat and Philoctetes puts the arrow in the quiver. He leans over the side of the boat and holds me tight.

The small box with the metal latch is gone. Philoctetes doesn't seem to care — his honor was bound up with the arrow, not with the mystery of the box. I am soothed. But the last of the fresh water is also lost, of course. We cannot waste time. He takes the oars and pushes and pulls with all his strength. In silent agreement, he follows me east until he collapses in sleep.

I swim the rest of the night, pulling the boat by a loosened thong. I fear no predators anymore — a result of immortality. But I fear the loose thongs. The boat looks as though it's been through a storm. If the planks come apart . . .

The return is slow, for Philoctetes runs out of strength too soon and his leg wound brings excruciating pain, even though I clean it repeatedly. It takes us almost three full days to reach Lemnos. Philoctetes is near death from lack of fresh water.

He never mentions building a boat again.

THIRTEEN

B
I
R
T
H

The gloom Philoctetes felt, the gloom that compelled him to build that boat, appears to be gone. But my own gloom grows. One morning, after breakfast, I drift off. I swim without goal. Soon, though, I find myself swimming quickly. I go in a jagged path all morning. I grow wild. Frantic.

Finally I hear what I instantly realize I sought: the hard blow of a male porpoise and the sighing blow of the three females near him. I head directly for them. I hear more males, more females, the whole enormous school.

I swim into the center of the pod. They leap high and change direction and speed along faster than any school of mermaids. I believe they are trying to lose me. But, while I cannot leap like them, I work hard to keep up. When they look at my humanlike arms and fishlike scales, I look right back at them, unapologetic. Eventually they accept my presence; they slow down.

At first I am disoriented by their chaotic noises underwater — clicks, creaks, barks, moans, sputters — and their grunts and whistles above water. But the sounds gradually become familiar, even pleasing. I mimic them.

The porpoises are interested in me now. They nudge me in their curiosity. A young female shyly rubs along the full length of my back and rushes away. I rush after her and rub back. We spin around each other as we move through the water.

And now the adults frolic, too. They leap again, but not to get away from me, just for pleasure. They make graceful arcs in the air. They tease passing fish by pulling their tails. They are playful, mischievous, familiar. How I miss my rowdy sisters, my school.

We feed on mackerel, eating in a similar fashion: We chomp on the fish with our teeth, then swallow them whole. I think of how Philoctetes rubs the scales off fish with a sharp stone, how he later pulls the bones from their baked flesh. It is good for a moment to eat normally, naturally again.

We swim leisurely. The afternoon passes.

Noises come from behind. The commotion grows. The porpoises circle, tense but not frightened. I move with them, trying to understand. A large female swims clumsily in the center. She twists side to side. She calls to the others continually and they call back. Another female stays at her side, moving along the length of her, rubbing gently like the young female rubbed me before. The large female writhes harder.

Oh. I see now. I see the small tail that emerges from the hole on her underside. The baby wriggles out tailfirst. I am full of joy. The baby is the length of my arm — so dear. A few spiky hairs protrude from its snout. I want to touch it.

But the porpoises are noisy in a different way now. The baby seems stunned. It drifts. Even I know that it needs to shoot quickly to the surface for a breath, or it will drown. The porpoises gather under the baby and push it upward. Hurry, I am saying inside my head, hurry, hurry. I swim at the edge of the circle, back and forth, back and forth. I rise with them.

The baby lolls on the surface. The adults poke at its side. It gasps, mouth wide open. Finally it whistles. The whole school bursts into celebratory dance. The infant nuzzles her mother and nurses. I have never felt more content.

We float. The sun sets and the porpoises sleep in the water, alternately swimming and bobbing with the waves. The newborn stays close to her mother's back fin, sound asleep, as well. But I cannot sleep. Mermaids don't have blubber to hold them up. If I fall asleep, I will sink. I swim back to Lemnos.

The beach is deserted, but the embers of the fire haven't yet died. Philoctetes has eaten and gone somewhere else to sleep. Does he miss me? Does he fear I will never return?

I go to my rock and sleep alone, like I slept in those weeks on Lemnos before I met Philoctetes. I think of the baby porpoise. Sadness comes from nowhere and weighs me down.

I will never belong to a mermaid school again.

I will never be a mother.

The next morning Philoctetes appears on the beach, where I await him. He kisses me and presents me with a breakfast of fruits. He doesn't ask where I went yesterday though his eyes show a flicker of worry.

"You are more respectful of privacy than any mermaid could ever be," I say as I tend to his wounded leg.

"I will listen if you want to talk, Sirena."

This is a reversal, for it is I who listens at mealtimes as he tells stories. Still, there are things he doesn't tell me. He didn't tell me how he spent his days all that time he was building the boat. And suddenly I remember another secret: "There was a box in the boat."

"What?"

"It got lost when the boat turned over. A box whose top was made of tiny squares."

"Mosaics. Don't you know mosaics?"

"No."

"Oh, Sirena." Philoctetes sits up. His face is all surprise, then he grins.

"Tell me about them."

"Not now. Someday perhaps you'll let me know about yesterday and someday, I don't know how long from now, I don't yet have a plan, but someday, Sirena, I promise I'll let you know about mosaics."

His promise quiets me. But only temporarily. Soon I am consumed once more with his lack of probing about yesterday, grateful and resentful at the same time and confused by both emotions. I promise myself to swim with porpoises once a year on the anniversary of yesterday — and I promise myself further not to tell Philoctetes where I have gone on that day and why. I understand neither promise.

FOURTEEN

D
E
B
A
T
E

The day begins with a cold drizzle. I have tended to Philoctetes' leg and we have eaten heartily. Now we sit on the sand.

Philoctetes' face is animated. "Everyone else is winning wars and killing ferocious beasts and —"

I turn away. I'm used to this kind of talk by now, for Philoctetes expresses envious wishes every spring. But today they irritate me.

He pinches my tail playfully. "Do you become bored with talk of heroes?"

"Heroes." I touch his face tenderly, but I can't keep the edge from my voice. "I wouldn't call the men who deserted you heroic."

"They aren't the best example of humankind."

"But you are. You are the Hero of Lemnos."

Philoctetes laughs. "There is no chance for heroic deeds on Lemnos. There is no chance to be honorable."

"You chased off the bear when she would eat me."

"That was long ago — years. Since you have become immortal, there are no more chances to save you."

"You live a decent, honest life. Is that not heroic?"

"Who could live otherwise on Lemnos?"

"Oh, Philoctetes, my hero. Each day is filled with little opportunities to give each other joy. You seize those opportunities and thereby show your honor."

"Sirena, my mermaid, you make so much of so little. Why, Heracles —"

"Not another tale of Heracles."

Philoctetes assumes a half-teasing look. "Do you become bored with me as well?"

"With you, never. With Heracles, perhaps. You know he's not my favorite."

"What about Theseus then?" Philoctetes' eyes glow. He loves Theseus almost as much as Heracles. He rubs his hands together in enthusiasm.

"Are you sure you have the time?" My words are peevish. I know I should bite my tongue, but I don't. "Lately you rush off so fast to this work of yours."

"The task before me now isn't easily done in the rain."

"Oh." I don't want to ask, but I can't stop myself. "Are you building another boat?"

"No. I'm working on . . . well, you'll see soon enough." He smiles mysteriously. "Theseus, yes. Let's talk of him. He was Heracles' cousin. I knew him well. I know many of his stories."

I, too, know many tales of Theseus, and not just the ones Philoctetes has told me. Amphitrite didn't have much appreciation of Theseus. Her tales come rushing from my memory. "Theseus killed all the bandits on his journey from his mother's home in southern Greece to his father's court in Athens."

"Yes." Philoctetes slaps his thighs. "A superb fellow."

I rise to the new debate that Philoctetes does not yet realize we have entered. "He hurled Sciron over a precipice."

Philoctetes nods affirmation. "The bandit Sciron would make his prisoners kneel to wash his feet, then kick them into the sea. It was a fitting end."

"He fastened Sinis to two pine trees bent to the ground, then let them go," I say.

Philoctetes is still nodding. "The bandit Sinis did the same to his victims."

"He made Procrustes lie upon an iron bed, then cut off parts of him till he fit the bed."

Philoctetes clasps his hands together. "Exactly the same method the bandit Procrustes himself used to kill those he robbed."

I try to keep the cunning from my voice. "Were not Sciron and Sinis and Procrustes dishonorable for employing these methods?"

"Of course they were."

"Then was not Theseus equally dishonorable?"

Philoctetes stands up in frustration. "You still don't understand honor." He plops down on the sand beside me again. "You don't understand the way humans look at it."

"Perhaps I don't."

"You need to, Sirena, if you are ever to understand me fully. It is right to reap the rewards of the seeds you yourself sow. These bandits deserved their end and Theseus was brave and glorious to render them their just rewards."

"Is there no room for pity among humans? No room for small acts of kindness?"

Philoctetes pulls on his beard. "Of course there is." He gets on his knees and with both arms he sweeps the sand into a mound before him. He works at the mound, digging out corridors, forming walls. At length he settles back on his heels and smiles. "I believe that's right."

I am curious about the sand structure Philoctetes has built. But I will not appear too eager. Part of our debate game is to show a certain loftiness. To feign lack of interest. I throw sand on the dying fire from our breakfast, then scatter the embers with a green log.

Philoctetes' eyes twinkle. I haven't fooled him for one minute. "I'll tell you a tale of Crete, so you will understand how Theseus showed his kindness."

I tilt my head in approval. "Is that sand structure part of the tale?"

Philoctetes nods and smiles. "Minos ruled Crete for many years. His son Androgeus visited Athens, where King Aegeus, the father of Theseus, received him. But Aegeus made a terrible error: He overestimated the youth's strength. He sent Androgeus on a dangerous expedition — with orders to kill a bull. But the bull killed Androgeus."

I sigh. This story reminds me of many others. Humans, it seems, persist in inadvertently causing the death of the young of other humans.

"Minos invaded Athens in his rage and demanded that every nine years the people of Athens should send him seven maidens and seven youths, all of them pure of heart and body, to be eaten by the Minotaur — otherwise, he would burn the city of Athens to the ground."

This was a fitting retribution for his son's being killed due to the poor judgment of King Aegeus? The invasion of a whole city? The threat to wipe out all its inhabitants? I lower my brow, but hold silent.

"The Minotaur was a monster, half bull, half human."

What? I tense up, every nerve tingling. A hybrid? Philoctetes has never told me a tale of hybrids before. I didn't realize there were other hybrids besides us — the mermaids. I don't like Philoctetes talking about a hybrid monster. I want him to hush. But at the same time I need him to talk.

"The god Poseidon had given a beautiful bull to Minos for Minos to sacrifice to him. But Minos couldn't bear to kill such a magnificent creature. To punish Minos, Poseidon made Minos' wife, Pasiphaë, fall passionately in love with the bull."

"And they mated?" I am astounded by the logistics of it. The woman should have been crushed by the bull's body.

"Yes. And Pasiphaë gave birth to the monster."

"Describe him," I say, fighting to keep the urgency from my voice. I want to know Philoctetes' true feelings about this hybrid — and he may not be so forthcoming if he senses my intensity. "Describe the Minotaur."

"He was a bull, a great and powerful animal, and where his neck should have been rose the torso of a man. A handsome man, they say, but for the horns on his head."

Very much like me, I am thinking. The bottom is animal, the top is human. The Minotaur was a combination of a cud-chewer and a normal human. "And why," I ask casually, as though the question is of no great import, "why would this bull-man want to eat people?"

"Why? I have no idea. He must have been full of rage and hate."

"Rage and hate at whom?" I ask. "At his mother? At Poseidon?"

"I don't know, Sirena. It doesn't matter. The point is that King Minos had Daedalus, a master architect, build a series of walled-in paths that were so intricate that no one could find their way out of them. They covered great areas of land, with mountains and fields. He called the structure the Labyrinth. Minos kept the Minotaur in the middle of the Labyrinth and every nine years, when the fourteen young people of Athens came to Crete to be sacrificed, he sent them into the Labyrinth, whence none of them ever escaped."

"Did the Minotaur ever eat people in front of anyone?"

"What?"

"How do they know he ate people? Did they see him do it?"

"I don't know, Sirena."

"How could he live on food just once every nine years? Did he have a way to preserve the flesh?" For without that, I am thinking, I do not believe he lived on human flesh. I believe he grazed grass, like other bulls, or gathered nuts and fruits from trees, like other humans. He was a hybrid, an innocent — not a monster.

Philoctetes shakes his head in annoyance. "How he managed to live on those few sacrifices doesn't matter. What matters is that one year Theseus volunteered to be one of the sacrificed youths of Athens. And when he went to Crete, the daughter of Minos, Ariadne, fell in love with him. She got Daedalus to tell Theseus the secret of how to get out of the Labyrinth."

"A secret passage?"

"No. It was simple. Theseus merely carried a ball of twine and unraveled it as he went." Philoctetes smiles as though what he is about to say is clever beyond words. "To get out, all he had to do was follow the twine."

"An idiot could have thought of that solution."

Philoctetes looks at me oddly. "You keep missing the point, Sirena. Don't you see? Theseus didn't know when he left Athens that he could ever find his way out of the Labyrinth. He went to Crete on a journey of immense peril to kill the Minotaur so that no more innocent young people would perish."

"And he killed the Minotaur."

"He slew it in its sleep."

"A sword against a defenseless animal."

"Theseus went without weapons. The Minotaur's horns were sharp. He broke one off and stabbed the beast."

I look away, overcome by anger, yet not convinced of its righteousness. Certainly if fourteen Athenians went into the Labyrinth every nine years and none ever came out, it was possible that the Minotaur had eaten them. But it was also possible he had not. Perhaps they simply got lost. People are stupid about retracing their steps — this much I've learned from knowing Philoctetes. Birds and fish, even land animals, do much better. Perhaps Daedalus, the architect who was cunning enough to construct the Labyrinth from which no human could find an escape, was the unwitting murderer here.

"So you see, Theseus was brave beyond measure. He risked his life to spare the lives of those young people. He showed enormous kindness." Philoctetes lies back in the sand. "The drizzle has stopped. We can swim now if you like."

I look up as if to study the sky. "Are there other creatures like that?"

"Creatures? What do you mean?"

I say the word as plainly as I can, with no trace of misery. "Monsters. Are there other monsters like the Minotaur? Half one creature and half another?"

Philoctetes finally understands. He sits up and touches my shoulder. "The Minotaur was not a monster because he was part bull and part man. He was a monster because he ate people."

I brush off Philoctetes' hand. "You are quick to believe evil of this hybrid when you've seen no evidence of the evil."

Philoctetes shakes his head. "I'm sure there was evidence."

I do not dignify his words with a retort. "Tell me. Are there others?"

Philoctetes' face grows dark. "Another Theseus story deals with such . . . creatures — hybrids — the Centaurs."

"Describe the Centaurs," I say firmly.

"Horses, horses up to their necks, then the torsos of men, just like the Minotaur." He looks at me with steady eyes.

"And did Theseus slay all of them, as well?" My voice is bitter.

"No. He drove them out of the country of the Lapithae."

"For what reason? Were they accused of being human-eaters, too?" I almost spit the words at him.

"They were related to the bride of Pirithous, the king. They —"

I push on Philoctetes' shoulder. "What? Are all the hybrid creatures of the world related to royalty?"

Philoctetes grabs my wrist before I can push him again. His face is flushed. "Do you want to know what happened or not?"

I close my lips hard and nod. His hand still circles my wrist. He trembles with emotion, and I find myself yielding already. I love this man for his strength of feelings. I cannot stay angry at him.

"The Centaurs came to the royal wedding. But they got drunk and —"

"Drunk?" I imagine these half-horse, half-men creatures, reeling around a wedding. Clanking into things. I look at Philoctetes and I see he is imagining the scene as well.

He grins sheepishly, in acknowledgment of the ludicrous picture. He lets go of my wrist. "Quite a spectacle they must have made."

I can't help but give back a small smile. "So what did they do in their drunken stupor?"

Philoctetes becomes serious. "They tried to rape all the women."

Rape. I think of Little Iris, my mother, and Eros, my father. "All right," I say in defeat. "All right. I'm glad Theseus drove them away."

Philoctetes takes a lock of my hair from each side of my head and follows their curls with his palms. "Sirena, I don't know if all hybrid creatures are related to royalty, but I do know that not all hybrids are monsters."

"There are yet others? Tell me about them."

"Shall I tell you the story of the charming mermaid?"

I laugh. "Let's swim."

FIFTEEN

THE GIFT

"Come." Philoctetes kicks sand over our breakfast fire.

"You're not going inland to work?"

He grins. "Today we spend together. All day long." He walks along the beach. "Get in the water. Let's go."

I roll into the water and call, "Where are we going?"

"To the stream."

"Why don't you swim with me?"

"I'm going to be in the water too long today as it is. You'll see."

"Is this a good surprise?"

"I hope it will be the best surprise."

I laugh in delight. "Then you cut through the woods. That's faster. I'll wait for you at the mouth of the stream."

Philoctetes takes off at a run. I swim fast. A surprise. The best surprise. I reach the stream and swirl in the great rush of water.

"Swim upstream," Philoctetes calls from the bank.

I swim with great effort. The stream is always widest, highest, fastest at this time of year. It is truly a river now. I could never swim any distance against this current if I were still mortal, for I'd run out of energy almost immediately.

Philoctetes strides along the bank, looking over at me regularly, his face alight with happiness.

"How far?"

"A ways yet."

The stream's source is high up in the mountain. Already the angle of the streambed grows sharper. It is hard work to keep up with Philoctetes. His step bounces with excitement. My own heart beats faster. A surprise lies ahead.

He breaks into a run. And soon he stops, fists on hips, and looks at me triumphantly. At his feet is a stone wall.

I swim to the side and touch the rough stones curiously. "Did you build this wall into the bank?"

"None other."

"But why?"

For answer, he lifts a large stone from the top of the wall and sets it aside. Then another. He works steadily, dismantling the wall. He whistles as he lugs the stones aside.

"You built a wall only to take it down? You're very mad," I say.

"Move downstream a ways, Sirena."

"Why?"

"You'll see. Just do it. Fast."

I swim away, and none too soon. The stream bursts through the weakened wall, tumbling the stones backward. It gushes over. And now I see a huge trench on the other side. I swim to the opening and let the water carry me into the trench. I am swept along in the wild current.

Philoctetes races on the land to keep up.

The trench leads downhill and away from the stream, to an inner part of the island. Ahead I see the houses. I didn't realize there were so many houses on Lemnos. It must have been a bustling town, after all. The trench goes straight to the building in the center. I recognize it as a temple, for Thetis' wedding took place outside a temple of exactly the same shape, with the same columns at the entrance.

The water washes me into the temple. And now I

swim around the dark, cool inside. I go underwater. The floor of the temple has been dug out and a new set of paving stones lies deep enough below the ground level that I can swim comfortably in this pool. I surface.

Philoctetes swims beside me. "Do you like it?"

"You dug that long trench? And you dug out this floor? And put in the new stones?"

He smiles and swims in circles around me.

"Why isn't the water seeping out into the ground?"

"I filled every crack with the shell-and-pine-resin mix that I devised for that boat so long ago. It works well, don't you think?"

"So much work. You did so much work, Philoctetes. Why?"

He swims to the opening of the temple and climbs out onto the land. Then he disappears. A few moments later, the bright light of morning pours through.

I look up at the window. And now Philoctetes takes a hide off another window. And another. The sun sparkles off the water inside the temple. The reflection sparkles off the walls.

The walls! They are covered with tiny tiles, all in vibrant colors. The colors show scenes. A maiden rides on the back of a bull. In the air, Eros watches. And beside them in the sea, Poseidon rides a porpoise. It is the rape of

Europa by Zeus, who turned himself into that bull. And while I cannot understand the glory of that tale, I have to marvel at the beauty of the woman, the bull, the sea, the sky, everything.

My eyes wander from scene to scene. Here is Hephaestus holding an ax with which he has just cleft the forehead of Zeus. Athena, armed but not yet fully grown, emerges from her father's head. And here is the Titan Rhea, presenting to her husband Cronus a swaddling cloth that holds a stone instead of the baby Zeus. She saved her son from his father — just as Mother Dora saved the mermaids from Rhodope. I follow the scenes around the room. "All of them are homages to Zeus."

I spoke to myself, but Philoctetes answers, for he has returned to my side. "Yes. This temple is in Zeus' honor."

"It's stunning."

He kisses my cheek. "Finally you know the wonder of mosaics."

"Oh, thank you." I throw my arms around his neck and kiss him with all my love. "The little box in the boat so long ago — did its cover hold a mosaic about Zeus?"

"Not Zeus. Its cover showed the infant Heracles strangling the serpents Hera sent to kill him in his cradle."

"Oh." I understand why it was so important to him —

yes, for Philoctetes, too, battles one of Hera's serpents every day, as that wound refesters. I hug him tight.

"The best is yet to come." Philoctetes swims to an altar tablet. It rises from the water, its face to the ceiling. He pulls himself up so his forearms rest on the tablet. "Look."

I pull myself up, too. Now I gaze on the mosaic of the tablet. It is a scene beyond my imaginings. A hideous rock looms from swirling waters — but it is not a rock at all. It is a woman with snakes and dog heads growing from her very body. She is ugly beyond belief and her face is filled with horror. In the sea a man looks up at her, his eyes radiating love. But he, too, is not what he seems at first. For a fishtail emerges from the water behind him. "A merman."

"Glaucus. Have you never heard of him?"

"Never."

"He was a fisherman. One day he caught many fish and dropped them on the grass beside him while he baited his hook anew. The fish suddenly wriggled all the way across the grass and jumped into the sea again. Glaucus knew the grass was special. He reached down and ate some. A terrific desire seized him and he plunged into the sea, refusing to come out. The god of the sea accepted him and turned him into a merman."

A merman. A merman, and Mother Dora never told us anything about him. "Does he live still?"

"I don't know."

"And why does he love this monstrous woman-rock?"

"You can see he loves her, can't you? It's so clear in his face. She was the nymph Scylla. He fell in love with her as she bathed, but she considered him a monster and ran away. So Glaucus went to the magician Circe for a love potion to feed Scylla. But Circe fell in love with Glaucus and, instead of helping him, she poured a poison in Scylla's bathing water. The poison turned her into a true monster. She stands as a rock in the sea, full of loathing and fury. She wrecks all ships that come close enough to her."

"But Glaucus loves her all the same?"

"He knows what happened to her. He feels responsible. He loves her for who she was and what she cannot control. He is loyal." Philoctetes presses his shoulder against mine. "He is a hybrid, Sirena, like you. And he is no monster."

My eyes cloud with tears for sadness at Glaucus' ill-fated love. Still, Philoctetes' words are so good, so good. "Why did the people of Lemnos put this mosaic of Glaucus in Zeus' temple?"

"They didn't. I did. I found it on the wall of the bath-house. I chipped it out and built it here, for you."

I finger the tiles lightly. "So many of them. Oh, Philoctetes, it must have taken you ages."

He strokes my hair. "It was worth every minute." He pulls himself up onto the tablet. Then he lifts me onto him. We intertwine on the altar of doomed love.

Immortality

PART IV

SIXTEEN

T
H
E
G
A
R
D
E
N

Bear Beach has become our special place. It is the beach where the house with the walled-in garden stands. In that walled-in garden, Philoctetes and I first kissed. I love Bear Beach.

We are in the garden at Bear Beach today, working side by side. We have decided to make this garden whole again, to restore it to the beauty it once had, long ago, before the people of Lemnos condemned themselves. I don't know why we didn't think of this sooner. Spring flowers would have been a welcome treat, a needed treat, for spring always brings a period when Philoctetes' leg wound festers much worse and his fever rages. It is Hera's annual reminder.

I work happily now. It is my job to find and bring back the kinds of water plants that can flourish in this fountain. I visited the rushes in the river nearby. I even swam upstream to a quiet pond. The water lilies will bloom white with a yellow center. The water iris will also be yellow. A small stirring in my center surprises me. As a hybrid, I cannot reproduce, yet the desire is unmistakable. If I were fertile, I know now that spring would have been my spawning time. Now it makes sense that it is spring, always spring, when I need to go away and swim in a porpoise school. Sorrow coats me.

Yet the plants hold a consolation. They can bloom for me. They can color my world. And I will visit the temple later today. I'm sure that the trench is full to the brim, after its dry spell all winter. It's time to swim there and bask in the colors of the mosaics.

I turn now to the bamboo. They will have tan, feathery fronds in the fall. And the water hyacinth will be purple. I arrange them so the colors will mix, purple threading its way through the yellow and white.

Philoctetes takes responsibility for the land plants, though I work with him often. I want to learn all their names. I want to learn to recognize them by their leaves and flowers, just as he does. He is a tender man, to know the flora so well. I glance over at him. He sniffs a root in his hand, as though he anticipates the bloom already.

I, too, look forward to the aromas of each season. Some of the flowers in this garden grow from bulbs that still struggle to make their way up through the weeds that overtook this good land years ago. Some that should be bushy are spindly from fighting for a spot in the sun. I leave my water plants and roll across the dirt until I lie by Philoctetes' knees. I cup a pale green spike. "Will it survive?"

Philoctetes runs a finger along my jawline. "It will thrive. Gardens are resilient. Gardens are a source of strength."

"Strength?" I say.

"Whenever you doubt the forces that be, all you have to do is enter a garden."

I am troubled by his words. I have moments of longing, yes, but not of doubt. For all these years with Philoctetes, life has been good — so very, very good. Now I remember the failed boat we built. I think back to our debates about honor. Poor Philoctetes harbors doubts I cannot help him with. All I can do is love him.

My fingers scrabble in the dirt to free a white daisy.

SEVENTEEN

C
R
O
N
U
S

I am stringing dried starfish into a necklace. I haven't adorned myself since the cursèd day when two ships were wrecked on the underwater ridge off Anthemoëssa. But after my last visit with porpoises, I came back not just with the idea of digging a garden, but with a strange desire to decorate myself. I have been collecting these starfish ever since. They are small and delicate.

I feel the brush of lips on my shoulder. I turn and kiss Philoctetes full on the mouth. "Sweet husband, look." I hold up the half-finished necklace.

He nods in sleepy admiration, for he has just awakened from a nap. We are on a rock far off the shore of Lemnos. The water all about us dances brightly in the sunlight. Philoctetes taps the unfinished necklace so that it swings between my hands. "What's the occasion?"

I smile. "Just a feeling. I love beautiful things. Colorful things."

Suddenly Philoctetes sits up straight. "Ah." His eyes are aglow. "I have a surprise."

"Not another trench?"

"Nothing great like that. A small treasure." He lifts an eyebrow teasingly and grins. "Wait here, my love." He swims to the beach and disappears.

I string the rest of the starfish. Then I lie back and wait. I wait a long while.

Philoctetes flops a hide bag up onto the rock. In all this time he has never mastered balancing bowls on his head as he swims. But he has sewn himself a sturdy bag from deerskin and he places that on his head, with the drawstring between his teeth, just in case it should fall in the water. That way he can bring things out to whatever rock we decide to sit on.

I watch as he opens the bag. His smile is broad. His hands move quickly. He chuckles under his breath. I laugh at his enthusiasm.

Philoctetes holds out a green box.

I touch it gingerly. The sides are smooth and I realize it is similar to the latched box that fell into the sea when the manta rays upset our boat years ago — the box with the Heracles mosaic. "What's it made of?"

"Glass."

"Really? It seems so fancy."

"It was made by a master glassblower. You can tell by the clarity." He takes the box, holds it up to the sunlight, and points. "And by the precision of the corners." He turns the box around for me to admire, then places it back in my hands. "I've collected a few things that must have all been made by the same person. I'll show them to you later, if you like. Open it."

"A secret collection?" I am saying, trying to hold off the silly anxiety. Philoctetes shows me the things he finds: amphoras and chalices and bowls. But of course he doesn't show me everything. Of course.

"It's not secret. It's just little things."

"Where do you keep it?"

"Open the box, Sirena."

I unlatch the box. It is filled with spider silk that forms a cushion for a bright green scarab. I touch the shell softly with just one fingertip. It has been preserved with something that makes it shine.

"Green box, green beetle." Philoctetes takes my right hand and kisses the fingertips. "To match the greens of your tail. It brings luck, the scarab." He laughs. "As if you need it."

I hold the scarab up. The sun plays over it in a thousand sparkles. I turn the beetle this way and that, like Philoctetes turned the box. I want to show him I appreciate it. My husband collects beautiful things he's found in human houses. He has brought me this lovely gift. It makes my starfish necklace look puny and plain. I should be grateful. I should at least act grateful.

"Well? Don't you like it?"

Why does he have a private collection? I shake my head at the nasty doubts. "Thank you." I turn and nuzzle his cheek. "Do you truly have many treasures?"

"I don't know if they're all treasures. But I love things, Sirena."

I think of his name. "Philoctetes" means "lover of possessions." Does he realize he lives the destiny of his name? And, oh, there is consolation in that, at least: He collects these baubles only because his name forces him to, not because of any more serious need. "Where do you keep all your things?"

He points. I follow his finger to the cave at the top of the high peak on Lemnos. "In my home."

His home. The word hurts profoundly. Philoctetes has a home where I have never been. I blink the burn from my eyes. "A cave isn't a home."

"Yes, it is. I won't live in a human house."

I'm glad of that, at least. "Why not?"

"It hurts too much. It makes me miss that other life."

I place the scarab carefully on the spider silk and hold the box tight, trying to squeeze away the knowledge of his longing for humans.

"It fits me as a home, too." Philoctetes shakes his shaggy head. "See how bearlike I have become? A bear lived there before I drove it out. Maybe even the bear that threatened you in our garden at Bear Beach."

I shake my own head and argue, more to cover my pain than anything else. "A cave is dark."

Philoctetes shrugs. "I like it. When I talk, my words repeat in the deep hollows."

"Echo," I say. I put the box down and clasp my hands together. "Echo lives in your home. She's another of Hera's victims. Like you." Like me? I am wondering.

Philoctetes' face goes solemn. We usually avoid talking of Hera, but I know neither of us goes long without thinking about her. Philoctetes moves close to me now and encircles my body with his legs. "I am not Hera's victim, Sirena. She has cursed me with this interminable wound, but we have found a way to live with it. I am not reduced, like poor Echo." His eyes are true. His voice is sweet. He is right.

My tension finally releases. "Philoctetes, thank you for the box. Thank you for the scarab."

Philoctetes stretches out, lays his head in my lap, and smiles up at me.

"What's that in your hair?" I say.

"What?" Philoctetes sits up again and shakes his head hard. Then he bows in front of me. "Is it gone?"

The silver strand holds fast. My heart falls. I quickly set my face into a smile. "Yes."

"Good." Philoctetes slides off the rock. "I feel like dove for supper. How about you?"

I look at him, distracted. "Dove? Of course."

He swims back to shore.

I toss the necklace into the sea and lie back. I rub the sides of the glass box. I've been worrying about his calling a cave his home and his collecting baubles — two such harmless acts — when something of real import — a problem that won't go away — was before my eyes: Philoctetes has a gray hair.

In every other way he looks the same as the day I met him. He is muscular and wide and still quite young. His teeth are strong; the whites of his eyes are clear. He is a beautiful man.

Philoctetes has a gray hair. I know what this means.

Mother Dora explained to us the way humans change color as they approach death. I have thought of this moment on and off ever since that night in Philoctetes' boat, when he talked of how he would grow weak and bent. Up until now, I have managed to look only at his present state and ignore the future. But I cannot ignore it any longer.

I wedge the box into a crevice in the rock. Then I roll on my stomach and feel the warmth of the rock on my cheek and chest. I stretch out my arms and cling to the rock. I wish I could hold it, squeeze it, hang on forever.

Philoctetes has a gray hair.

He ages, day by day. I do not.

I swim in these waters without a thought for my own safety. I have had very little cause to be concerned about Philoctetes's safety, either. I can defend him in the water, certainly, but no sea creature is stupid enough to threaten him once they realize his great size. And Philoctetes is more than capable of defending himself on land.

We have found a life that suits us both.

But this gray hair is something else. Cronus, a relentless foe, has finally called the challenge. Philoctetes' precious bow and arrows are useless against Father Time.

All these years.

I don't even know how many. After a while, they just seemed to roll along, a continuous thread, strong and unbreakable.

But a decade from now and a decade from then — what? What then? I know I will love him, no matter how gray, how weak, how bent he grows. That is not the problem. Oh, if only it were.

How many years does Philoctetes have left? How many years will we have each other?

I sit up. No! I won't let him die. Anything can change. Anything can happen. If immortality was given to me, it can be given to him, too. Lovely Eos, the goddess of the dawn, fell in love with a human, too. She went to Zeus himself, the supreme ruler, and begged him to make her lover Tithonus immortal. And Zeus agreed. Oh, it didn't go well. Eos forgot to ask for eternal youth, so poor Tithonus withered away until he was nothing more than a creaky voice — the noise of a grasshopper on a summer night. But I will learn from Eos' plight; my request won't go awry.

I swim quickly to shore. Philoctetes is not in sight. Waiting has never been easy for me. I swim about the cove randomly. My head is full of shadows of thoughts. I cannot focus. Anxiety disperses my energies, my mind.

Philoctetes finally appears with two doves. He grins.

"I collected hazelnuts." He has always treated the hazelnut as a token of our marriage, since it was hazelnuts I fed him in his first real island meal. His presentation of the pile of hazelnuts in his pouch now is a prelude to our lovemaking. He is carefree. "Shall we stuff the doves before I roast them?"

I sit on the sand and shake my head. "Philoctetes, I must go away for a while."

"Away?" He looks at me dumbfounded. He drops the doves and sits in front of me. "But you just went away last month."

"This is different," I say.

"How long will you be gone?"

"I don't know. A few days. Not long."

Philoctetes looks at his feet. "Why?"

"I cannot tell you yet. Be careful."

He looks up at me and nods. I can see he is trying to understand. After all these years, I almost know his thoughts. "Does this have to do with your fish half?"

I am startled at the question. I had not guessed Philoctetes' thoughts at all. Philoctetes wonders what secrets I hold — whether I am subject to piscine rhythms and urges unknown to him — things similar to his need to collect human treasures. All along he has kept his wonderings to himself — showing respect for a part of me he feels he cannot understand. I am overcome with gratitude for his discretion. I want to tell him he can stop wondering. I want to tell him he knows everything important about me. I want to finally explain about my day each spring with the porpoises. How foolish I was not to tell him. But this is not the moment for revelation. Not as I am about to leave him for a task that must remain a mystery to him. I shake my head. "I cannot talk about it. Not yet." Maybe never, I think. If I fail, then I will never mention my attempt to Philoctetes.

Philoctetes straightens one leg and kicks at the doves mindlessly. Then he gives a slow, shy smile. "You be careful, too."

His warning is a game; he knows I cannot come to harm. My ever-playful husband. I smile back. "You know I will," I say.

He whispers, "Come back, Sirena."

"Oh!" I embrace him. "Never doubt that. Just take care of your leg every morning. Do exactly what I always do." How many days can he survive without me if the wound festers badly? I will hurry. I must. "And eat well. Get enough sleep."

Philoctetes smooths my hair. "I will."

He seems suddenly small in his humanness, in his mortality. I speak with my cheek pressed against his shoulder. "Maybe you should sleep in the cave up on the hill, in your home."

He holds me at arm's length so he can look into my face. He smiles. "I'll sleep in the garden at Bear Beach, surrounded by flowers you have planted." He pulls me to him again and we embrace hard and long.

EIGHTEEN

D
O
R
A

I have no hesitation as to where to go and I have no elaborate plan. I will simply ask for help. I swim night and day, never tiring, never flagging.

When I arrive at the bay, I know Mother Dora is waiting for me. I feel it. I dive and enter the underwater grotto where I sat for so many storytelling sessions.

Mother Dora sits on a rock and looks at me, as beautiful and regal as when I saw her last. The giant sea turtle stares at me from behind her.

I want to swim into Mother Dora's arms. I want to

cling and beg. Instead, I observe the decorum that is customary in her presence. "Fair Dora," I say. I sit on the sandy floor at her feet.

Mother Dora leans forward and takes my face in both hands. She kisses my forehead. "You are more lovely than ever, Sirena. Your return brings gladness to my heart."

"I am glad to be with you, too." I hug her legs that I used to envy so much. Then I sit back. "Dora, Mother Dora, I need your help."

"Tell me."

I look in her eyes and see a scene — it is a scene of a mermaid on a rock with a man lying, his head in her lap. Mother Dora knows. There is no need to explain. "He must become immortal."

Mother Dora straightens and walks back and forth. She opens her hands to me in a gesture of futility.

I quell my immediate alarm. Surely I can appeal to her logic. I am used to debate from my arguings with Philoctetes. "Nothing is beyond your powers, Mother Dora. You could do it."

Mother Dora shakes her head.

"Of course you could," I say, but I am confused. She does not argue. This seems not to be a matter of logic. I must appeal to her affection for me. "You could do this for me, one of your mermaids. You are a goddess."

"No god or goddess would dare to intervene." Mother Dora shakes her head. "Hera hates him."

Hera the hateful. I swim to Mother Dora. "How can Hera bring so much misery? Isn't she also the goddess of marriage? I have a marriage, Mother Dora. Help me save it."

Mother Dora wrings her hands. "I cannot go against my queen."

"You are my queen, Mother Dora. You are as good as a mother to me. Please, oh, please, help me."

Her face is full of anguish. "No."

The word deafens me. I half expected it even as I swam from Lemnos to this grotto, yet it still thunders. "Is that your final answer?"

Mother Dora doesn't move.

"I could go to Hera herself."

Mother Dora looks at me with leaden eyes.

"I could beg Zeus for mercy. He showed mercy to Eos. Surely —"

"No." Mother Dora shakes her head. "You went against Hera's wishes when you tended to Philoctetes' wound. You could have lost everything then. Immortality. Everything. But I interceded on your behalf. I asked her to allow you to make love with him." Mother Dora cannot conceal the pride in her voice — or perhaps she does not try. "Hera's anger dies slowly, Sirena, if ever. We all know that. Zeus knows that best. He would never embroil himself in this mess."

"There must be some way."

"There is nothing left to do."

I swim in circles of desperation. Then I grab hold of Mother Dora's hands on an impulse. "Please." I hang on for dear life as I speak the words I didn't even dare to think when I was swimming here. "Make me mortal again."

Mother Dora looks at me with shock on her face. "How can you ask such a thing?" She pulls her hands away. "Do you know what you want to give up?"

"When first we mated, immortality seemed the perfect gift — it was wonderful. But things changed." I am shaking my head. "What good is living forever if he dies?"

"That's a ridiculous question. A moonstruck, romantic question. I am ashamed of you, Sirena."

"I don't want to be so different from him. I'm not asking you to make me human. I have accepted the form I inhabit and Philoctetes has, as well. But being immortal makes me much more distant from him than being a mermaid. I want to spend old age together with Philoctetes, understanding what each day means to one another."

"Each day means almost nothing, Sirena. You speak foolishly. Immortality is everything."

"What is immortality?"

"Foreverness. It is being here, there, anywhere you like, forever and ever and ever. For eons. It is seeing all things, and experiencing all things."

"Over and over and over again," I say.

"Yes, exactly." Mother Dora beams at me.

"Does it get better with each repetition, Mother Dora?" I reach for her hands again, but she pulls back before I can touch her. Her face is wary. "Tell me," I insist. Mother Dora walks and I swim behind her, persistent. "Is the hundredth scallop that much sweeter than the tenth?" She stops and looks at me. For a moment I think she will answer, but she does not. I press on. "Is the thousandth water lily that much more aromatic than the hundredth?" My questions demand answers. Mother Dora cannot just stand there, looking appalled. She must answer me. Someone must answer me. "Is the millionth love that much more tender than the thousandth?"

Mother Dora takes me in her arms and I struggle and struggle, then yield as though dissolving in these waters, knowing the fight is not with her. "Oh, my poor Sirena. How could you do it? How could you let yourself love a mortal?" She plays with my hair. "Where did these feelings come from?" She sighs. "Fish don't love. That half of you couldn't be the source. And gods never truly love humans. Some of us engage in lustful acts with them, but that's all. So the god half of you couldn't be the source."

I find my voice with difficulty. "Eos loved Tithonus."

"Flighty Eos. She loved Orion, too, and see where that got her."

"Oenone loved Paris."

"You make the point so well — don't you see? Such relationships are inevitably destroyed. Oh, Sirena, why must you always be the odd one? Why must you love so true?"

I bury my head in the curve of her neck. My sobs are soft. I am full of joy and sorrow at once. I love Philoctetes. True love. How could I not be joyful?

Mother Dora plaits my hair as she talks gently. "Dear Sirena, dear, dear Sirena. You know the rule as well as I: A gift once bestowed by a god can never be taken away. Rhodope gave all the mermaids immortality at the moment they succeeded in getting a man to love them. You are immortal now. No one can change that."

I pull back and look into Mother Dora's eyes again. This time I see no scene. She does not hold answers, after all. "Rhodope could."

Mother Dora looks confused. "How?"

"She could change the gift. She could say that if I love him, my mortality returns."

Mother Dora shakes her head. "The conditions were set long ago. Even Rhodope cannot alter them."

I swim around Mother Dora with renewed determination. "There has to be a way."

Mother Dora does not look at me.

"There has to be."

Mother Dora stands silent.

I swim in circles until I am so dizzy, I fall to the sandy bottom of the grotto.

Mother Dora kneels beside me. "Give him up, Sirena. Stay here with me." Her voice gathers momentum. I know she wants to catch me up in that momentum. "You can come with me on my inspections of both this sea and the Friendly Sea. We can visit all the rivers. You can see your sisters again, all forty-eight of them."

"My sisters?" I have missed my sisters. There is a hollow place of pain in my soul that I have not attended to in all these years. My sisters, the playmates I grew up with, the friends I shared all my dreams with. "Are they well?"

"Very well."

I hesitate. Then I ask the awful question. "Are they immortal?"

"Yes."

I want to scream. How many men died to give my sisters immortality? Oh, dreaded Rhodope. Oh, wretched sisters. I turn my face so Mother Dora cannot see my expression. "Give them my love."

"No, Sirena. Do it yourself. Stay with me." Mother Dora plaits my hair again. "The seas are full of marvels, things that even you haven't dared to imagine. You, Sirena, the one who loves to discover new creatures, new places. The one who thrills at new adventures. Come with me."

I shake my head. "I must go."

"You can ride the turtle into the wide open ocean."

I look at her sharply. Mother Dora knew my desire of so long ago. How much does she know? How much does she invade my mind as the aggressor, not the nurturer?

I remember the words of the song we mermaids used to sing. We promised the sailors that if they would come to us, they'd know all the past, know all the future. But we never meant to keep that promise. We weren't capable of keeping it. I know only that much of the past that Mother Dora and Amphitrite and Philoctetes have told me in stories. I know nothing of the future. Our song was a sham. We didn't think about it then. We sang what Mother Dora told us to sing, grateful for the words, grateful for the permission not to think. An utter sham.

Is Mother Dora a sham?

I swim for the opening of the grotto.

"Wait. What's the hurry? You have all the time in the world."

"Yes," I say sadly. "But Philoctetes does not."

CHOICES

PART V

NINETEEN

GREEKS

I am diving in the deep blue sea, where the waters run cold, far out from our home beach. I am escaping the heat of summer. Philoctetes is off in the woods that grow thickest at this time of year, hunting for our supper. I imagine him covered with sweat. He will swim with me later. I surface, intending to dive again, when I see the ship.

My heart becomes a cold lump.

Humans.

I cannot take my eyes off that ship. It comes from the east and heads directly for Lemnos. It is a battleship, just like the ship that brought Philoctetes to Lemnos. Is the Trojan war finally over? Are these men going home to Greece?

The ship comes quickly. My heart beats again, as though in rhythm with the bobbing of the distant topsail.

Given its present angle and the slant of the wind, that ship might well anchor at the south side cove, sheltered by bluffs. I could meet Philoctetes at our usual beach after his hunt and suggest we eat over in our garden near Bear Beach tonight. If the ship left quickly in the morning, Philoctetes might never see it. He might not know that humans had come. They could be gone as though they'd never been here.

Leaving no trace.

No harm.

Except the knowledge in my heart that I had deceived my husband.

I don't allow myself to think further. I swim quickly to our beach. I pick up the conch shell we use for a horn in times of danger and I blow as hard as I can.

Philoctetes appears moments later, crashing through the underbrush, his bow in one hand, an arrow in the other. "What is it, Sirena? What?"

I point.

From here the ship is barely visible on the horizon.

Philoctetes stares. Then he looks at me. "They will stop for fresh water and leave." He puts the arrow back in his quiver.

I nod. That is what I wanted to hear him say. He won't go with them. He doesn't miss the company of humans, after all. Humans abandoned him. He lives here now, with me.

"But, Sirena, you must stay out of sight. They might . . . they might not understand."

"You're right."

"I will talk with them."

Why? I want to say. I remember the night on his boat, when he tried to explain to me why he wanted to return to Greece. Can he still think that I won't love him in his old age? Can he still have such foolish fears?

But my chance to ask has passed. Philoctetes walks the coastline to the southern cove. I swim there. Normally Philoctetes swims with me when we go such a short distance, for he has adapted to water well, whereas I can never adapt to land. As he walks now, I wonder if each step reminds him he is human. I wonder if that is why he chose to walk. My heart jitters.

All of a sudden, my husband runs inland. I search for him anxiously. When he reappears at last, I gasp. He has put on the clothes he wore when he first came to Lemnos. He has had no need of them for these many years. But now he wears them. He looks strangely unfamiliar to me. The skin of my arms and chest prickles cold in the summer heat.

We wait, Philoctetes on the shore and me behind the rock. I tap the rock with all my fingers. I stroke it. I hug it. I feel lost.

The ship moves slowly, steadily, hatefully. Why must it come here, to Lemnos? The east sea, from Troy to Lemnos, is speckled with islands that offer fresh water. It should have anchored elsewhere. It could still go off course. If a wind arose. A storm. Oh, something. Oh, let them leave us be.

But the ship comes inexorably to Lemnos. Closer and closer. There is no doubt that Lemnos is its goal.

Finally it is here.

It drops anchor. Two men climb ropes down over the side and wade to shore.

Philoctetes stands tall. He holds the mighty bow of Heracles in his left hand.

The men approach him. I cannot hear their words. They talk for a long time. Now they embrace. They embrace, just as I used to embrace my sisters. They walk off into the woods, all three of them. I cannot know what they do. I cannot understand this reconciliation.

I swim underwater out to the ship and surface close to it, so close that no sailor on the ship could see me past the curve of the bow, even if he leaned over the side. My whole body pulses with fear. I hold tight to the ship and listen.

The sailors speak loudly.

"Alive yet. I can hardly believe it."

"Never heard of a man who survived the sea serpent's bite."

"Perhaps he's not a man. He looks like an animal, with that wild hair."

"Well, he's been alone, lame and in pain, for nigh onto ten years. You'd expect even worse."

"I wager he can't wait to get home."

"To a decent meal."

"To a soft bed."

"To an even softer woman."

The sailors laugh.

"Home. Let's make this infernal war end soon, so we can all get home again."

"Here's to that."

The sailors cheer.

I dive and swim to the rock. The wind wafts hot. I

know I should swim out, back to where I was when I first sighted the ship. I should dive and cool myself and explore the waters and keep myself busy. I should not hide here behind the rock, consumed by my fears, dwelling on the sailors' words. Yet, I cannot take my eyes from the beach. I keep hoping that Philoctetes will appear, that the men will fill their water barrels and take leave. Time crawls.

Does Philoctetes dream of a decent meal, a soft bed? Does he long for a soft woman?

Soft thighs.

One of the men appears on the beach. He is older than Philoctetes, although he is still in the prime of life. He splashes through the water out to the ship. He climbs on board.

I cannot resist, despite the fact that there are so many men on deck now and the danger of being seen heightens. I swim back to my spot at the point where the bow of the ship meets the water. I press against the wood of the ship and listen.

"So where is he, Odysseus?" comes one sailor's voice.

"Can't be taking the time to gather his many possessions, can he?" says another.

The sailors laugh.

"Did he kiss your feet in gratitude, Odysseus?"

"No, none of that." Odysseus' is a measured voice, one that shows he is used to giving commands. The other sailors are quiet, hanging on his words. "This ass has taken a strange liking to Lemnos."

"What? Is he insane?"

"He must be a lunatic."

"He is genuinely attached to the island, though I can't imagine why," says Odysseus. "He beds down in a cave, like an animal."

"He looks like an animal."

"What will we do?"

"Neoptolemus is working on him now," says Odysseus. "He will gain Philoctetes' sympathies."

"And if he doesn't?"

"If he doesn't," says Odysseus firmly, "it doesn't matter. We will leave with Heracles' bow and arrows. The stubborn blockhead can rot here if he chooses."

"Yes," the sailors agree. "Yes, yes."

I duck and swim back to the rock. The one called Odysseus is crafty and deceitful. The scoundrel would steal my love's bow and arrows. But his words ring in my ears: Philoctetes has become genuinely attached to this island. Oh, beautiful words.

I wait and watch the shore. The young man whom I now know as Neoptolemus comes onto the beach and wades out to the ship. He carries Philoctetes' bow and quiver — the precious gifts from Heracles, the tokens of friendship and honor.

Philoctetes stands on the beach and calls after him, "Stay on board during the night. Bears roam the beaches of Lemnos." He shouts it again, looking straight at the rock I hide behind. "Bears roam the beaches." He walks back into the woods.

I understand: Philoctetes is going to our walled-in garden at Bear Beach. He wants me to meet him there. I swim fast.

I move over the ground to the garden, feeling vulnerable, a sensation that is strange to me after these years of immortality. I wonder if the she-bear that stalked me so long ago lives still. I remember the thread of drool hanging from her mouth. My own mouth dries with terror. I want to scrape away this feeling. I want to shed my body.

But I realize that would not help, for the terror is not of damage to my body, but to my soul. Already I have heard in my head the songs of my childhood. Already, the powers I possess to seduce and hold captive rise to my aid. I could keep Philoctetes here on Lemnos if I sang. I could seduce him a second time. The first time I did it unwittingly — I sang to the she-bear to save my own life. It was an accident that Philoctetes heard; it was an accident that I seduced him. But if I sang again now, no such excuse could be given: My songs would be with cunning and deceit. I would be no better than the monster Odysseus. I don't want to sing. Mother Dora was right; I love Philoctetes true. Yet the melodies are loud in my head.

I go into the garden and Philoctetes closes the gate behind me. His face is ashen. His eyes burn. I go to the fountain and sit on its side and wait. He has much to tell me and I want to know it all, no matter what it is. I curl my tongue backward against the roof of my mouth to keep it from singing.

"They want me to go to Troy with them."

This I knew. I nod.

"The famous soothsayer Calchas has prophesied that the Greeks cannot win the war without me."

I remember Odysseus' knavish words. "Without you?"

Philoctetes chews his bottom lip. "No. Without the bow and arrows of Heracles."

"And so you gave them the bow and arrows?"

"Yes. Neoptolemus thinks he stole them at Odysseus' bidding. He asked to take care of them for a while. He has no intention of returning them." Philoctetes takes a deep breath. "I let him think I was fooled."

I shake my head. "The bow and arrows belong to you. You loved their owner. You cannot let these men take them." You cannot let them take your honor, I am thinking. Though I have never agreed with Philoctetes' view of honor, I know he cannot bear such a loss.

"The choice is the bow and arrows alone, or with me as well."

I hate the choice. I know Philoctetes hates it. I am grateful that he hates it. I wish desperately that we could let it go at that. That we could be joined in the hatred of a choice Philoctetes was forced to make.

But Philoctetes does not let it end there; his face works with emotion. He speaks at last, heavy words. "Neoptolemus is the son of a friend of mine."

So friendship enters here, as well. A cold sheet of dread spreads on my chest like the funeral shroud Philoctetes wrapped Heracles in. Humans do much, risk much, for friendship. They give their very life. I know this from every word in every tale Philoctetes has told me of his adventures with Heracles.

"His father was killed by Paris in this unending war."

"Paris." Anger bubbles out of me like lava from a volcano. "That fool started the whole war, and for nothing better than desire of a beautiful woman."

"Not just a beautiful woman, Sirena. Helen is glorious. I saw her once. I stood among her suitors in Sparta."

My Philoctetes courted Helen? I am silent. Philoctetes has a past I have seen only hints of. He was enamored of a human woman whose beauty causes men and gods alike to behave as though they are demented. This man before me yields himself to the same carnal attractions as all others. The revelation should be no surprise, yet it estranges me from him. I am floating away on this revelation, farther and farther out to sea. I had thought Philoctetes loved me, all of me, the fish of me as well as the woman of me. Now I am lost. This is what comes of seduction.

"Neoptolemus wants me to come to Troy and kill Paris. He wants me to avenge the death of his father."

His words reel me in quickly. I will not simply give up and become a memory — not for something so base as this. "Vengeance," I say with heat, "think of vengeance, Philoctetes. Was it not Hera's vengeance that caused so much anguish for Heracles? Is it not that vengeance that causes so much anguish for you?" And for me, I am thinking. "Vengeance is the worst of emotions."

"His father was a great warrior, a champion among men. In our small time together this afternoon, I heard many tales of his bravery against the enemy. Tales of valor." Philoctetes pauses. He pulls on his chin hair. "Neoptolemus tells me the Trojan ground now streams with the blood of Greeks and that it will grow into a river unless I come."

"Neoptolemus stole your bow and arrows. He is not to be trusted."

"I gave them to him."

"But he thought he was stealing them. It's all the same, Philoctetes. He is not worthy of trust."

"He is the only son of my friend."

I look into the tormented eyes of Philoctetes and pray he will not speak the words I know he must speak next.

"I am tempted to go to Troy, Sirena. But if I go, who knows what will happen?"

Exactly my thoughts.

"I owe them nothing, Sirena. My fellow countrymen abandoned me here." He clears a spot among the evening primrose and sits down. "My own people deserted me in my hour of need. They didn't know you would come and care for me. For all they knew, I would die of the serpent bite or be eaten by leopards. They didn't care. Why should I care about their damned war, about rivers of Greek blood?" He drops his face in his hands.

And now I am imagining the tales Neoptolemus must have told Philoctetes about his father's courage. I know very well that Philoctetes wishes such tales would be told about him. After all, Philoctetes revels in the power of stories every single day of our lives together. This is honor to him, true honor — to be the main character in a tale of courage. I cannot pretend not to know this.

"They don't deserve my help. And if I left, Sirena, if I left . . ."

What? What is he thinking? "Are you afraid you might die?"

Philoctetes laughs bitterly. "Afraid of death? No, I will die sooner or later. What difference does it make, given the eternity in which I will have no part? What I fear is that I'll live but never get back to you."

Our eyes hold each other, but I do not move into his embrace. The dilemma confounds me. I feel unsure of anything. I need to gather the pieces of myself. Philoctetes doesn't insist. We retreat through the black silent waters to our rock.

"I am weary," he whispers. He falls asleep beside me, his breaths warm, rhythmic.

I do not want Philoctetes to go to war. Yes, he must die someday. Still, if he stays here with me, at least he can live a long life. It matters not that Philoctetes is enchanted, rather than in love. Whatever the cause, he is undeniably part of me — for he himself told Odysseus he is attached to this island. I do not want him dead on a battlefield.

But this is my fear, not Philoctetes'. He wants to go to war. I see it in his eyes. I hear it in the timbre of his voice. He wants to use his beloved bow and arrows for the honor of his dead friend.

His real fear is that if he goes to war and survives, he might not return. He might choose a different life.

My husband needs to go and I stand in his way.

I feel the stars. Each sparkle sets aflame the pain in my heart.

TWENTY

VENGEANCE

I will not think any longer about Philoctetes' need to be with humans. Those thoughts lead down an ever-narrowing path of pain. I stare at the summer constellations of Ursa Major and Ursa Minor. The brightest tonight is Sagittarius, the archer. I concentrate on the archer. It is fitting. I tell myself the constellation tale for comfort. I say it in the voice of Amphitrite.

"Come," says the voice of Amphitrite. "Come, my mermaid friend."

My thoughts are talking to me. They are so real I feel as though I've actually heard her voice.

"Hurry, Sirena."

I sit up and look around.

Amphitrite is here, on the rock. I am not sleeping. This is no dream. She commands again, "Come with me. They await us." She dives.

I follow. We swim along the shallow bottom to a circle of underwater rocks where the starlight reaches. A nymph perches on each rock. I stand in the center beside Amphitrite and look around, bewildered and awed at the sight. The nymphs say their names one by one as my eyes light on them.

Pherusa. Dexamene. Callianira. And, oh, the fair Dynamene. Melite. Iaera. The ox-eyed Halia, and Actaea the fair. Callianassa and Nemertes and the faithful Apseudes. The widely renowned Galatea and Clymene. Ianassa. Maera.

I am much less than halfway around the circle when my eyes stop at Thetis — Thetis, whom I know so well. She comes forward. "Neoptolemus is my grandson."

"Oh," I cry. The friend Philoctetes spoke of was her perfect son Achilles. The friend whose heroic feats he lauds. Oh, poor Thetis: Her son's death calls Philoctetes to Troy. I hug her in her grief. But even as I hold her tight, I know that this is one more intrigue to clutter the path and obscure the route to escape. The trap is sprung.

"For the honor of my son Achilles," says Thetis, drawing herself back from me, "for the honor of the most valiant warrior of all time, Philoctetes must go to Troy."

I am not offered the chance to respond, for now Oenone steps forward. "Paris the treacherous, who killed my sister's son, ruined my happiness forever."

Philoctetes has been called upon to kill Paris. Paris the treacherous.

Oenone wails. "Honor. My honor. Achilles' honor. The honor of Greece."

"What is honor?" I look from Oenone to Thetis. I will not be fooled into accepting their deceit out of sympathy with their misery. Their misery cannot justify mine. "Your cry is for revenge. I see no honor in it."

"Look harder," says Thetis. "You are letting yourself see only what you want to see."

It is not I but they who see only what they want to see. I search for reasons they can hear. "But if he leaves me —"

"Hush." Mother Dora is now beside me. "Don't argue, Sirena. You have a decision to make. It is the most important decision you will ever make."

"I have a decision to make? Is this another seduction? When has any of it been up to me?"

Mother Dora's lips are thinly closed. She waits.

I look around the circle again. Why have all these nymphs assembled here, together? "Why do you pretend to need my cooperation?"

The nymphs mimic Mother Dora.

I turn to Mother Dora in desperation. "If Philoctetes leaves me, he will die of the serpent bite."

"He didn't die when you came to me to ask for his immortality." Mother Dora pats my hair as though with affection. "He was alone for several days and he didn't die."

I move out from under her hand. "He stayed on the beach, near the curing salt water. If he goes into the battlefield in Troy, the infection will win. He will die without having the chance to avenge anyone."

Mother Dora shakes her head. "Heracles will be disappointed if Philoctetes doesn't try."

"Heracles is dead."

"Heracles talks to Philoctetes now, even as we speak."

"Heracles is dead!" I am shouting.

Mother Dora's face is unperturbed, as though I haven't said a word. "He has made the difficult journey from Hades' realm for no purpose other than to convince Philoctetes to do the right thing."

The gods care so much that they have allowed Heracles to leave the underworld? Why? "What makes this war the right thing?"

Mother Dora ignores me. "Heracles promises Philoctetes that he will send Machaon to Troy to heal him." Mother Dora smiles across the group of nymphs. "Machaon is the son of Asclepius and, like his father, an excellent physician." The nymphs nod in agreement.

"Why should Hera allow Machaon to heal him?" My tone is defiant.

"Hera cannot prevent other forces from intervening. Ah, I see the future now . . ." Mother Dora looks at me slyly. ". . . if you let it happen, dear Sirena. I see wine washing the wound. I see healing herbs and the serpentine stone. I see Machaon cutting away rotten flesh and only new, healthy flesh growing in its place. A permanent cure. Or as permanent as cures can be for humans." Her eyes turn hard. "If he stays with you, I see only daily rot and stench and pain."

Philoctetes has pain from his leg, I cannot deny this. Yet I won't accede so easily. "All the Greeks need is the bow and arrows. Surely Neoptolemus can kill Paris with Heracles' bow and arrows."

Thetis takes my right hand. "Philoctetes is a bowman like none other. His first arrow will go wide. The second will strike Paris in the bow hand. The third will strike him in the right eye. The fourth will strike him in the ankle. There will be no need of a fifth."

Oenone lets out a small shriek of grief. Even in her hatred of Paris she cannot forget their past love. Mother Dora encircles her shoulders with one arm. Mother Dora, the pillar of strength. And I wonder again if Mother Dora isn't as deserving of hatred as anyone. Yet, like Oenone, I cannot forget our history — the years of her kindness when I was young and ignorant.

I turn to Mother Dora with the knowledge that she is relentless in her own way. It is over. Thetis spoke not what anyone here wishes, but the actual future — she spoke what will be. It is truly over. There is only one thing I do not know. "You, Mother Dora, you know how Philoctetes will be healed. Thetis knows how Paris will be killed. I, too, need knowledge."

"Ask, Sirena."

"I must know what will happen to Philoctetes after he kills Paris."

Mother Dora shakes her head.

"But I must know."

"You are immortal, Sirena. But not even the gods can know their own future."

"It is Philoctetes' future I want to know."

"What is the difference, dear Sirena?"

That answer can be interpreted so many ways. I search for a retort that will make her stumble and reveal our future against her will. Someone tugs my hair. I swing around.

"Now you'll know what it feels like to lose a lover," says Rhodope, horrible Rhodope, who appears as if born of my own fears. I realize she must have hidden behind the others so that I wouldn't see her. She was biding her time. She doesn't even try to mask the savagery in her voice. Her face is as beautiful and hard as I remember it from so long ago. "It's your turn now."

"But it's not the same thing." I lift my chest in battle. Why should I spare Rhodope when she has been the cause of so many tears? I speak cruel words: "You were betrayed. But Philoctetes leaves me for honor, not for another lover."

"Stupid pride." Rhodope laughs. I recognize her laughter. I heard it after Philoctetes kissed me that first time. I heard it when I labored with Philoctetes in the cordgrass, building his ill-fated boat. It is a ragged laugh. "Don't you think he knows human women await him after the war? Do you really think he doesn't dream about that, Sirena?" Rhodope turns to Mother Dora. "Mother, didn't you talk about Sirena's worries? Didn't you say she's been comparing her scaly tail to soft thighs?"

Mother Dora glares at Rhodope. "Violence does not become you. Sirena is already convinced of what she must do."

Rhodope laughs again and turns back to me. "You know what he really wants. You'll know the pain. Oh, yes, you'll know." She swims off, her laughter trailing behind.

The other nymphs have broken into clusters. They look away in embarrassment from the brutality they've just witnessed. I want to call to them. My humiliation at Rhodope's hand doesn't matter. Mother Dora hasn't given me the information I sought. That's what matters. This meeting isn't finished. I want the nymphs' attention, their support.

But Thetis still holds my right hand. And Amphitrite now takes my left. They force me away. The nymphs call out in farewell from every direction. Their voices ride the currents.

TWENTY-ONE

L
O
V
E

Philoctetes kisses the sleep from my eyes. We slip off the rock together and I take care of his wound, just as if this were a morning like any other morning. We are playing a game. I have been visited in the night by the sea nymphs. Philoctetes has been visited in the night by Heracles. Our lives are changed forever. Yet we pretend it isn't so. We eat raw clams, a taste I have taught Philoctetes. Then he climbs on the rock to wait and I hide behind it. We do not speak. There is neither need nor point.

The ship has not departed overnight. It could have

gone. The men had what they wanted. But there it is. I knew it would be there.

Now it is my job to make Philoctetes depart on that ship. My job to do the opposite of what my heart most desires.

Neoptolemus climbs off the ship and wades through the water to the cove. He wears the bow and quiver of Heracles over one shoulder. He calls out. I wonder what new treachery he plans.

Philoctetes dives off the rock and swims to the cove. They talk. They hug. I do not know what is sincere and what is not. Neoptolemus returns the bow and quiver to Philoctetes and goes back to the ship. Philoctetes swims to our rock. He stays in the water and calls to me. "Sirena."

I come out from my hiding place.

"Neoptolemus is honorable, after all. When he realized that Odysseus meant to leave without me, he refused to keep up the hoax. They fought bitterly." Philoctetes' voice is triumphant. "The young man has the spirit and decency of his father, my friend Achilles. Indeed, Neoptolemus himself is my friend. He gave me back the bow and arrows."

"I saw." I touch the bow, which Philoctetes has draped across his chest. This is the first time I have seen him wear his bow and quiver in the water. I recognize the significance; he has donned his old role. I look at him for confirmation, but his eyes still glow with the knowledge that Neoptolemus has proven himself honorable after all. That young man has decided not to trick Philoctetes, just as I decided not to deceive him so long ago. But Philoctetes' actions are controlled by other forces, in spite of Neoptolemus' honesty — just as Philoctetes' enchantment with me was beyond my control. Neoptolemus and I are both ineffectual. I should feel an affinity for Neoptolemus. Instead, I feel only the slow strangulation of the bond of their friendship.

"Last night in my sleep, Heracles came to me." Philoctetes pauses, waiting for my reaction. His face is filled with expression. He hopes I will feel joy for him that Heracles came all the way back from Hades' realm to advise him. He hopes I will celebrate with him the strength of their friendship.

But no, this I won't do. At last I let all my sadness show. What point is there in keeping pretenses any longer? Philoctetes must go. We both know that. It is my responsibility to keep him from faltering, but it is not my responsibility to act happy about it. I do not stop my tears from falling.

Philoctetes brushes my cheek lightly. "Heracles asked me to go to Troy as a favor to him. He told me the Greeks would win and I would prevail. He told me to align myself with Neoptolemus and together we could bring fame and glory to Greece."

"So you will survive the war," I say softly. Blessed news comes from an unwanted source.

"Yes. And Heracles told me to take spoils of the war home to Greece, and give part to his funeral pyre and part to my father Poeas."

Home to Greece. Neither my arms nor the cave on Lemnos' peak are a true home for this man. I wipe away my tears and speak as if thinking aloud: "So you will return to Greece, not to Lemnos."

"That is the plan." Philoctetes takes a deep breath. "But, Sirena, I won't go at all if you don't want me to."

I hear the tremor in his voice. Going will pain him, but staying would kill him. "Those are hollow words, Philoctetes. If you did not go, you would hate me forever."

"I could never hate you, Sirena. I will love you for the rest of my life."

My head spins. Too many forces act at once. "They manipulate us, Philoctetes."

"Not if we do what we want."

Such innocent words. He has no idea of his own enchantment. I must disabuse him. My cheeks are on fire. "Philoctetes, tell me." I stop. And now I realize, oh pitiful me, how much I still secretly harbor the hope that no seduction ever occurred. If I pursue the question on my tongue now, I may forever destroy that hope. But I must know. And there will be no future chances to ask. "When did you first think you loved me?"

"I loved you from the first moment I saw you."

"No, that isn't so. You didn't even believe I was real when you first saw me. Tell me, Philoctetes. Think hard."

He is silent.

The silence is unbearable. I take the risk of prejudicing his answer. "Was it when you heard me sing to the bear?"

Philoctetes nods. "I loved your singing, yes. I have never understood why you steadfastly refused to sing again in all these years. Your voice is heavenly." My heart begins to bleed. "But that wasn't the start of my love for you. It was earlier, a few days earlier, when you built the fire for the first time. Do you remember? Do you remember smacking the flint together? Wonder and rapture crossed your face — the triumph and gaiety of innocence radiated from your soul. You even clapped your hands. In that moment, I knew I loved you."

I swim into Philoctetes' arms. Philoctetes loves me. And I love him. And the love is real and true. No matter how long or brief be life, love is invincible. Now I know why Mother Dora pressed on me to make Philoctetes go to Troy: She needed me, after all. The gods cannot break us apart — the gods cannot manipulate us — for nothing can affect a bond of true love. It is within my power to stop Philoctetes from leaving — for love gives me that power. And it is within my power to release him from the duties of love. I choose the latter — not for vengeance or any mistaken sense of honor — but for the good of the man I love.

Philoctetes tilts my chin up and looks into my eyes. "After the war, after I have played out my part in Greece, I'll come back to Lemnos."

"No." I shake my head. "You shouldn't leave humanity behind a second time. Live among people, Philoctetes. Take every opportunity for honor and glory."

Philoctetes' eyes shine wet. "My love for you transfixes every part of my being. I am not whole without you." He pulls one arrow from his quiver. "Love creates a whole. So long as you keep this arrow, my honor is intact."

We kiss this final time, our tears mingling as our cheeks touch.

I take the arrow and watch my love depart.